Henry Morford

Sprees and Splashes

SALZWASSER
VERLAG

Henry Morford

Sprees and Splashes

Reprint of the original, first published in 1863.

1st Edition 2022 | ISBN: 978-3-37500-193-3

Verlag (Publisher): Salzwasser Verlag GmbH, Zeilweg 44, 60439 Frankfurt, Deutschland
Vertretungsberechtigt (Authorized to represent): E. Roepke, Zeilweg 44, 60439 Frankfurt, Deutschland
Druck (Print): Books on Demand GmbH, In de Tarpen 42, 22848 Norderstedt, Deutschland

SPREES AND SPLASHES;

OR

DROLL RECOLLECTIONS OF TOWN AND COUNTRY.

A BOOK FOR RAILROAD RIDES AND ODD HALF-HOURS.

BY HENRY MORFORD.

NEW YORK:

MDCCCLXIII.

SEE STORY OF "BILLY RADFORD'S LOST PUP."

CONTENTS.

PREFACE.

In one respect this collection of sketches is believed to be different from any previous product of the American press—all the incidents related being personal to the writer, or within his knowledge to intimate acquaintances. No other excuse can be offered for the too frequent use of the pronoun "I" throughout the volume. Although some of the characters introduced have belonged to the rougher and less careful classes of society, whose words were not always picked and measured, care has been taken to use as few rough expressions as possible without sacrificing naturalness,—and none that could be offensive. Where well-known persons have been introduced, a thin veil has been drawn over their personality by slight changes of name, while the sound is generally near enough to enable friends to trace out the reality. Some of the sketches included have had circulation in various newspapers, while others have been written especially for this volume. It is hoped that both old and new may be found welcome visitors, in the present form, especially in those "odd half-hours" for which longer stories are not acceptable. The writer begs to return his warm acknowledgments to the press for courtesies extended in previous ventures, and for the very kind and generous manner in which this collection has been noticed in advance.

NEW YORK CITY, January, 1863.

SPREES AND SPLASHES.

I.

BILLY BURTON'S BOTHERATION;

OR,

TWO SELLS FOR ONE THEATRE.

PERHAPS the merriest winter of Burton's Theatre was the last of his personal management—the winter when Mathews, Brougham, Walcot, E. L. Davenport and his wife, Polly Marshall, Lizzie Weston Davenport, and all that jovial crew, played there. The shadow of managerial failure, though it had already loomed over Burton, had not yet settled upon him; and certainly no abler collection of stars and stock company was ever gathered, than that with which during that closing winter he fought the phantom.

Mathews had finished his round of performances and gone away to Boston, late in the season; but Brougham, Walcot and several others of the prominent actors yet lingered. The houses had been thin for a few days, and Burton felt the necessity of raising some description of excitement. In this he was seconded by Brougham, who had been playing with the manager for two or three evenings in

"An Unwarrantable Intrusion," which all play-goers will remember as a piece of pure nonsense by Brougham, in which an old hunks is intruded upon by his daughter's lover in disguise, the whole farce crowded full of gags, and more than half the dialogue in the mouth of each, shot at the audience instead of the other actor.

Taking a hint from the roars of laughter which had greeted this in its re-production, Brougham concluded to get up something original of the same character, but much more extensive and ten times more impudent. The result which followed a conference between Brougham and Burton on the subject, was that a new piece was underlined for production on the next Saturday evening, called: "This House to Be Sold." Naturally every one not in the secret supposed that the new piece, which was announced as a short one, was a farce having some kind of money-embarrassment of a house-owner, as the principal incident in its plot.

There was a good house on Saturday evening, partially drawn, there is no doubt, by the announcement of the novelty, which was understood to be by Brougham. I have forgotten what were the two pieces which preceded the new production, though I remember there were three on the bills besides the "fair rose and expectancy." The leading piece may probably have been Brougham's "Columbus," which never drew well, or Thomas Dunn English's "Life Among the Players," which neither drew well nor deserved to do so. However that may have been, the curtain went down on the second piece, and all the house waited half an hour or thereabouts for its rising on "This House to Be Sold."

At length the gods in the gallery began to stamp and "hi! hi!" a little, the intermission being a shade too long for their exacting tastes. Ten minutes longer of waiting, and the gods in the gallery were joined by the audience in the boxes and the parquette. They, too, were getting impatient. The stamping and shouts were changing into very decided marks of disapprobation, when the curtain was finally drawn back at the right, and Moore, the stage-manager, made his appearance in front, making a low bow to the audience. Silence was secured after a moment, and Moore, who seemed out of breath and flustered, was enabled to secure a hearing.

"Ladies and gentlemen, we are really under the necessity of begging your indulgence for a few moments longer. This piece has some very extensive and complicated machinery, and I am sorry to say that some of it has got temporarily out of order. If you will only be kind enough to wait a few moments longer, we think it can be arranged!" and with another bow Moore slid himself off again at the stage right, amid some applause at the explanation, a few expressions of impatience, and not a few cries from the boys in the galleries: "Come, hurry it up!" "Lummoxes!" "Up with that rag!" and other complimentary East-side adjurations and insinuations.

A few minutes more of waiting, with some noises and suppressed talking behind the curtain. Everybody began to get impatient, now, from the gallery gods to the gloved dandies in the boxes and the critical force in the front seats of the parquette. More stamping, "hi! hi!"-ing, a little shouting and a small proportion of muttering. A minute or two more and Moore once more made his appearance before the curtain, and again began to apologise. This time he was not quite so well received. A few hisses came, mingled with cries of "Oh, we've heard that before!" "Gas!" "If you're agoin' to raise the curtain, why don't you do it?" "Hurry up your cakes!" &c. Moore, in spite of the disturbance, began to say something like:

"Ladies and gentlemen, I am really very sorry—very sorry—more hindrance—things gone wrong—hope you will excuse—bye-and-bye," etc.; when out from the other side of the curtain rushed Walcot, his hair out of order, his face wearing a ludicrous affectation of alarm, and looking, generally, as if he had just been scared out of a brush-heap. He caught Moore by the arm and pulled him aside. By this time the audience began to be reasonably impatient, but even more puzzled, and dead silence fell, in the effort to hear what Walcot was trying to say in a low tone to Moore.

"Oh, we *must* do something!" the latter was heard to say.

"What *can* we do?" asked Walcot, in a tone pretendedly suppressed, but loud enough to be heard back several seats. "How *can* we go on if the author—"

"We *must!*" said Moore. "The audience have paid their money—"

"That's *so!*" roared out some enthusiastic individual who fancied he had heard what was not intended for his ears.

"Tell the audience," suggested Walcot.

"No, *you* tell them, if it has *got* to be done!" answered Moore.

Each hereupon tried to push the other forward and to fall back himself, for a minute or two, while the tumult in the house thickened and general dissatisfaction began to be pretty evident. Neither had yet said a word to the audience in explanation, when Brougham plunged suddenly out from behind the curtain at the stage right. He, too, had dishevelled hair, and looked as if there might have been a sort of general scrimmage behind the scenes, in which he had been considerably a sufferer. At sight of *him*—he being generally understood to be the author of the unfortunate piece, quiet fell once more; and John, rushing up to the footlights, and laying his hand on his natty waistcoat with a low bow, began to make an explanation something like the following, in a drawling, puffing voice, and the most Broughamy style imaginable:

"Ladies and gentlemen, I really don't know how to address you at this moment. I really don't, upon my soul. Such an unfortunate circumstance I never saw in the whole course of my life. We have here a most excellent piece—a wonderful piece, but we can't do anything, you know, of course we can't—without the piece itself. Unfortunately the author, who is the most timid and nervous man I ever saw in the whole course of my life, seems to have got angry at the little delay about the machinery, and he has gone off home."

"What of that?" said a young man in the parquette. "We don't want *him*. Go on with the piece!"

"That is the difficulty, ladies and gentlemen," said Brougham. "I never knew such a thing in the whole course of my life; but the play has been produced a little in a hurry, nobody knows it quite as he should do, and he has carried off the piece and all the parts in his pocket!"

At this announcement some only laughed, a few hissed, some others stamped, Brougham apparently became discouraged and mysteriously disappeared; while Moore and Walcot retained their places in front of the curtain, gesticulating to each other and muttering something that nobody could understand.

Now matters began to be seriously complicated

among the audience. Pretty well forward in the dress circle, on the audience-right, sat an eminently respectable-looking old man, white-headed and white-whiskered, and supporting his gloved hands on an immense gold-headed ebony cane. He looked as if he might once have been a military or naval officer—was evidently wealthy—and no more complete incarnation of propriety and respectability could have been imagined. By his side sat a pretty, bright-looking, dark-haired girl of eighteen or twenty, well-dressed, and apparently bearing the relation of a daughter to the old gentleman.

During all the delays, apologies and explanations, the old gentleman had been observed to be very nervous and fidgety, and once or twice he had only been restrained by the expostulations of the girl, who kept her hand confidingly on his arm, from getting up and making some kind of a demonstration. When Brougham made the announcement that the play could not go on because the author had eloped with the piece —the man with the white hair and whiskers could no longer be restrained even by the efforts of his handsome daughter. He started to his feet, his gold-headed cane firmly grasped in his right hand, and giving it an emphatic thump on the floor and clearing his throat with an emphasis which drew all eyes upon him, he broke out in a full clear tone which could be heard from parquette to gallery:

"If there is nobody else here to protest against this imposition, *I* do! I have paid my money to come here to see a play, and I don't mean to be put off with a row in the place of one."

All attention in the house was of course by this time withdrawn from the stage and concentrated on the stout old man, in spite of the fact that the group in front of the curtain had been increased by the presence of Manager Burton himself, who came out bare-headed, as if alarmed at the inexplicable imbroglio, and anxious to make some kind of an apology. But if the audience did not notice him, the old man in the boxes *did*, for he addressed his next remark directly to the manager.

"I call upon the manager of this theatre," he went on, holding up a bill of the performance in his left hand and slapping it with the cane in his right—"to put a stop to this most extraordinary proceeding. Here we are promised a play, sir!" and he looked square at Burton, "a play, and after we have paid our money to see it, and waited half an hour to have the curtain rise, we are informed that the author has carried off the play, and that we are only to have apologies. It's a swindle, sir! a swindle! the most disgraceful thing I ever saw!"

"Oh, do sit down!" cried the girl, evidently in trepidation, and pulling him by the arm.

"Officer!" sang out Burton, whose face had been working itself up to a terrible pitch of anger, "Officer! is there anyone to keep order up there in the boxes?"

As he asked the question a policeman entered the door of the box, immediately behind the excited paterfamilias, and approached him. Another was seen at no great distance behind, also approaching the scene of disturbance. The attention of the audience was now pretty equally divided between the interlocutors on the stage and in the box.

"Yes, sir, a *swindle!*" repeated the loud man in the box, decidedly, bringing down his cane on the floor with a thump that sounded over the whole house.

"Officer, take that man out!" cried Burton, from

the stage. In a moment, the hand of the first policeman was laid upon his collar.

"Take your hand off my collar!" cried the assaulted individual, enraged. "I have paid my money to come in here, and have a right to protest against this swindle."

Some cried "shame!" some "don't hurt him!" others "take him out!" in the midst of which general disturbance a man who looked and spoke marvellously like Pat Hearn, the odd and generous-hearted gambler who died three or four years ago—rose up in a private box to the audience left, and commenced an exordium both to Burton and the disturber, in that mixture of short jerk, mumble and nasal drawl, for which he was so well known during his later years.

"Oh don't, Burton, that's too bad, you know. It's a real shame—mumble—mumble—to take a fellah out when the play isn't done—mumble—mumble. Why can't you be still, you know?—mumble—mumble. Gad! what's the use of all this muss? Aha!—mumble—mumble," and so on until he seemed to be exhausted and subsided again into the corner of his box.

Meanwhile, after a short struggle on the part of the white-haired man to retain his seat in the box, he had been dragged away by the two policemen, and disappeared, accompanied by the girl. By this time Brougham had again made his appearance in front of the curtain, and in a short speech, terribly mixed up, between Brougham and Burton, the announcement was made that the play of "This House to be Sold" had been duly performed, the house having been really "sold" most effectually.

By this time, too, those who had not before been sufficiently well aware of the personality of the actors and up to the tricks of the Brougham repertoire, to understand the whole thing from the beginning—began to have an inkling of the truth. There was no play, and the "selling of the house" consisted in "selling" the *theatrical* "house" (audience), with the series of tricks and apparent blunders here recounted. The young man in the parquette was, if I remember correctly, Bishop, who afterwards played Uncle Pete at the Winter Garden; the old man in the box was Mark Smith, one of the best of stage old-men, magnificently got up for the purpose; the young lady who played his daughter was pretty little Miss Miller, who was so acceptable a member of the company during the latter part of Burton's management, and afterwards when the theatre became the Metropolitan; the counterfeit Pat Hearn in the private-box was Brougham, who had got himself up in a capital imitation of the gambler, and slipped in and slipped out again without being perceived; and the policemen were both stage counterfeits sent in front for the occasion.

The "House to be Sold" really went off very well; and the applause, on the first night, when the explanation had been given so that everybody knew exactly "where the laugh came in," was uproarious. Brougham and Burton felicitated themselves on "a hit," and though there was not much money in it, they had really made one.

II.

Near me, in the parquette, on that Saturday evening, sat a queer genius, connected with the newspaper and theatrical world of this city, whose name may be set down as Sam Long, from the fact that he might not thank me to be more explicit in the designation. He knew actors, actresses, stage and stage-tricks, as well as could be desired, and had burned his fingers—so report said,—in trying that gross impossibility—making money out of a theatrical manager. If he had a more especial passion than any other (people who pretend to know him best, say that he has not changed in that particular)—it was for a clear, well-defined, outrageous practical joke; and timid people who were aware of his proclivity sometimes steered clear of him to avoid the peril.

It is scarcely necessary to say (and that of course, is my principal reason for saying it) that both Sam and myself was well aware, before-hand, what "selling the house" was to be. Sam not only chuckled drily over the perplexity of the audience, but seemed at times to be doing a little private and extra chuckling on his own account. I remarked, when the affair was over, that it had gone off well—better than I had expected.

"Yes," said Sam, "but not half so well as it *can* be made to go off. See if I do not add a tail to that performance in a day or two, that will improve it remarkably!"

"How?" I asked.

"Never mind, now," answered Sam. "Too many people around at present to talk about it. Let me see—yes—drop in here again about Tuesday evening' if they keep on playing it, and see the after-piece."

I promised that I would do so, and we separated. I did drop in again on Tuesday evening, the "House to be Sold" being yet on the bills; and I saw the after-piece.

Sam had gone to work pretty extensively and with a good deal of judgment, in arranging his *dramatis personæ*. His first requirement was a good *green countryman*, and he had found him in the person of the good and brave little Charley L——, a master's mate in the United States Navy, who had done good service in the old Jamestown, who was then off duty in this city, and who afterwards caught the seeds of his death, which occurred only two years ago—bravely heading a company of the marine brigade in the march through the deadly swamps of Paraguay. Poor L—— was not only the best little fellow in the world, but he was also the gayest and the merriest. I have never known a better mimic—his comedy accomplishments having been put into hard training years before on the stage of the old Broadway, of which one of the most accomplished actresses (Mrs. Abbott,) was his near relative.

Second in the forces Sam Long had mustered for the occasion, was a clerk in a well-known book-house, named for this occasion, Hooper, who had not been so long absent from the country air in which he was born, as to have forgotten its rough drolleries. Then it seemed that Long had skimmed the down-town printing-offices for a dozen or two of reasonably well-dressed wild fellows, all of whom he had thoroughly drilled for their role of that evening. It afterwards appeared that he had made use of his acquaintance among the policemen, to have the captain of the precinct and one or two aids present in plain clothes, to guard against the possibility of a real riot growing out of his venturous operation, while the patrolmen on duty were properly tutored not to meddle unless there was absolute necessity.

All this was duly communicated to me by Long, when I reached the theatre on that evening. He had his reserve corps (the printers' boys) duly posted a little in the rear of the place where Mark Smith had his nightly position; while L—— and Hooper were to perform generally in the lower part of the house until the time for the catastrophe. Long held, I believe, some position at that time, in connection with the city government, and he had probably made known the sport in advance to so many of the officials as he judged to be "safe," for the parquette was dotted half over with well-known heads from the municipal and fire departments.

It was part of Long's plan, of course, that he should not be conspicuous. Inveterate scamps always adopt that precaution. He had accordingly taken his seat in the parquette, a few seats back from the orchestra, where he presented, for the time, the lugubriously sober appearance of a Methodist parson who had surreptitiously dodged into the theatre and was trying to escape observation. It was necessary that the two principal *actors* should make themselves conspicuous before all the house; and when I reached the theatre they were doing so at the top of their ability.

L——, dressed in an exaggerated Yankee suit that was almost too broad for deception, and playing the character as well as Joe Jefferson ever did in his life—was seated on the front seat of the parquette, staring at the ceiling, eyeing the house—mouth ludicrously opened and tongue going (when ever the curtain was down) in observations that might have been fresh from Wethersfield. This performance he varied by drafts on his exhaustless pockets of apples, candies and oranges, the debris of which lay around him like the gleanings after a harvest. Beside him sat Hooper, playing the character of the country bumpkin who had been half civilized by some years in the city, and explaining to his wondering companion all about the marvellous splendors of the house and what they were going to do when they pulled up that big curtain.

All the parties in the parquette, within hearing

of the Yankee blunderings of L—— and the whimsical instructions of Hooper, were smothered in laughter more than half the time during the intermission, and no small proportion of it during the playing of the first piece, which was, I believe, on this occasion, "Columbus." They were, consequently, in a good state of mental preparation for that which was to follow.

Finally the curtain went down on the opening piece, and the intentional blunders of the "House to be Sold" commenced. The reputation of the "sell" had now extended over the city, and probably all present, of their own knowledge or informed by others, were aware of the real character of the pretended malcontents among the audience. There was, consequently, none of the real unquiet and disturbance of the first evening, and everything would have passed off in the most unexceptionable manner, but—.

As the curtain went down on "Columbus" I saw that L—— and Hooper left their place in front of the parquette and strolled out, the impromptu Yankee gaping, if possible, more broadly than ever. Sam Long kept his position in the centre of the parquette. Mark Smith and Miss Miller had changed position for that evening, and come on the other side of the hou-e, but the "forces" had recognized them at once, and adroitly shifted ground to the lobby in the rear. Thither slowly wended L—— and Hooper, the Captain and Lieutenant, and thither I followed them at a distance.

Everything went off in the most stereotype order, up to the time of Mark Smith's rising to make his protest. I was then two or three seats away to the left, and had a fine opportunity for observation. L—— and Hooper had gradually edged down the aisle, very near to Smith, followed by the "recruits" and unobserved by the actors. L—— was apparently more gapingly verdant than ever, and scattered his "darns" and "goshes" with a looseness that was thoroughly refreshing to any one in the secret.

Mark, as the white-headed old gentleman, rose to deliver his protest, and slammed down his cane with due energy. Burton dodged out from behind the curtain and gave the order to the sham policeman to "take that man out." The policeman seized Mark by the collar and commenced to drag him towards the door, the assailed man commencing his protest, as usual, that "he had paid his money and was not going out." Not less to his surprise than to that of nearly all the others around him, he found a champion not bargained for in the programme.

"Paid his money? yes, I'll be darned if I didn't see him, and he ain't agoin' out o' here, neither!" broke out a strong nasal voice of the regular Wethersfield twang, and the small Yankee made a lunge at the other side of Smith from that grasped by the policeman, and attempted to hold him back.

"Don't, don't! let him take me out! it's all a joke!" cried Mark, who saw at once that some greenhorn must be deceived into a belief of the reality of the persecution, of course.

"Look a-here, boys, help a fellar, won't ye?" sung out L——, who had got hold of one of the big legs of Mark, and held him, the policeman still trying to drag him out, now assisted by the second. This appeal was answered by a forcible rush on the part of Hooper, shouting, "No you don't, policers! You ain't a-going to drag out folks wot's peaceable!" He made a lunge at the second policeman, stooping his head as he did so, and carried him off his legs. By this time the recruits had rushed down, and in the rush away went Mark and the first policeman on the floor, Miss Miller only being saved by the arm of a gentleman near, who drew her out of the melee. In a moment every person in the box was on foot in alarm, and almost at the same instant the audience sprung up in consternation all over the house. To outsiders the scene must have been fearful, and the prospect of a dangerous riot imminent. From my point of view nothing could be seen in the neighborhood of Mark and his assailants, but a heap of people squirming through and over each other, like a basket of very lively eels. Nobody was being hurt, of course, for that was not part of Sam Long's programme; but the whole affair looked immensely like it.

I had time, in the midst of my observation of the central picture, to catch a glimpse of two other points. On the stage stood Burton, white as a sheet, under the impression that his "sell" had been misunderstood, and that a riot had begun which would possibly cost some bloodshed and end in the demolition of his theatre. He was trying to make himself heard in explanation, but the house was Bedlam and he could not speak. John Brougham had forgotten his part of Pat Hearn, and rushed on the stage in the peculiar make-up of that character; while the noise had frightened all behind the curtain, and besides Moore and Walcot a dozen others were peeping out in that quarter.

My other glance of observation was directed at Sam Long. He stood calmly up in his place in the parquette, and surveyed the row in the boxes, with the air of saint and martyr.

At this stage of the proceedings, the sham row having gone far enough, the real police stepped in to prevent anything worse, and arrested L——, Hooper and two or three others, whom they took around into Mercer street and dismissed in safety.

Mark and Miss Miller had been rescued and carried away, and Burton had been able to make the explanation, which he still thought to be necessary, to the audience—that "the man in the boxes had not been put out, and the whole thing was a joke."

He was interrupted by Sam Long, who stood up in the parquette, pointed his finger at the manager, and roared out—

"Sold! The house is sold—*twice!*"

The roar of laughter which broke from all parts of the house, and a glimpse of Long's face, which he knew quite well enough for comfort, seemed to tell Burton the whole story. The stage in front of the curtain was clear in a moment.

Brougham, keen as he is generally, "didn't seem to see it." He left the theatre fully impressed with the fact that the piece had been performed a little too naturally, and that a genuine row had been the result. Perhaps he was undeceived by the receipt of the following epistle, which L—— was charitable enough to send him a few days after, and of which Sam Long yet retains a copy, at once as a trophy of one of his most successful practical jokes, and a memorial of the true-hearted young sailor:—

"MR. JOHN BROUGHAM:—Dear Sir: You don't appear to know it, but you are sold! You remarked, in conversation with a friend yesterday, that 'This House to be Sold' was performed so well on Tuesday evening, as really to threaten serious results, as some 'green countryman' bit at the bait, and attempted to prevent the expulsion of Mark Smith. It may be of interest for you to know that the 'green countryman' has known and laughed over the capital acting of Mark Smith, for years, as he has done at yours—and that there was not the least danger in the world of a row. All the affair was 'put up,' in revenge for all your atrocious theatrical villainies, and the public and the players are square. The 'house was sold,' and the auctioneers with it, at least on that evening.

"Yours truly,

"THE GREEN COUNTRYMAN."

And that is the way in which Billy Burton's "botheration" took place, and how his "House was Sold" twice on the same evening.

II.

OLD JOE BRAMBY.

QUEEREST among all the originals who have chanced to cross my way at one period or another, was Old Joe Bramby, of Bushy Hollow, whom I shall paint precisely as I remember to have seen and known him nearly a quarter of a century ago—it having been nearly that time since he felled his last tree and was himself felled by the axe of the great chopper, Death.

Old Joe was, as the last paragraph would indicate—a woodman, *i. e.*, one of those poor men who made their daily living by felling trees and cutting them up in cordwood for market—toiling a life long on lands not their own—living poorly—faring hardly—but seeming to feel no trouble beyond an axe of bad temper or an occasional decline in the price per cord for chopping. A little cabin on a half-acre clearing in the Jersey back-woods, built of pine clapboards, unceiled and miserably furnished, afforded him the home to which he retired with weary limbs and aching back, when the sun went down on his labor. A wife with the perpetual sick-headache and a frock of inevitable blue-calico, and half a dozen slattern children equally bareheaded and barefooted, made up his domestic jewels—jewels that would scarcely have been riches to one differently born and nurtured.

An original in appearance was Joe—short and broad-framed, but thin, wiry and athletic, with skin tanned by exposure until it resembled a bowl of red earthen; one shoulder drooped lower than the other —he said, from carrying the axe so much, when going to and from his work, while others alleged that he had crushed down the lower shoulder with the logs of cordwood and fence-rails that he had "hooked," and carried home to his cabin after dark; gray hair and bushy eye-brows (when I knew him,) and a cast in one eye, which always gave him the appearance of looking in two directions at once and quizzing every one to whom he spoke.

No hero of romance was old Joe Bramby in his dress, for in winter it was the coarse home-spun, and in summer the cheap cotton drilling, which suited his limited purse; and his rough tarpaulin hat, the fancy for which he had no doubt caught from some relative who followed the sea—and his coarse boots, which were always patched, before thrown away, until, like the Yankee's jack-knife, the original was almost if not entirely lost—these were not changed, as were the leaves, at the advent of every spring and fall, but always did duty till sun, and storm, and hardship had brought them fairly to wreck and ruin.

Yet a hero was Joe, and one widely known over the country. He had probably caused more broad horse-laughs than any other man of his day; and his very appearance, even before he opened his mouth to speak, was often the signal for a guffaw of anticipation.

Two things old Joe Bramby did in perfection. In the first place he stuttered—not painfully to the hearer, as so many men do, when one can scarcely resist the temptation to procure a stick and pry the imprisoned word out of the laboring mouth—but calmly, slowly and beautifully. His language, in fact, would have lacked half the charm without the admixture of halt, jerk and stammer, which sent the words rolling out of his mouth like little pellets of drollery, tumbling over each other like kittens at play, and provoking a laugh on the gravest faces.

The second of Joe's qualifications, and the one without which the other would have been as incomplete and useless as half a pair of scissors—was his talent for *romance*. Let it not be supposed that he *lied*, according to the proper acceptation of that word—told falsehoods with the wish and intention of having them believed, and thereby producing a deception. Nothing of this did old Joe—his coarse, manly character would have revolted at the idea. But he had an imagination which would have made his fortune, had he lived in the days of Cobb, Southworth and Ned Buntline, and gone into the business of depicting scenes that never took place on the earth. He merely *romanced*—exaggerated everything he attempted to tell—so whimsically and outrageously that deception was as impossible as unthought-of.

"Where have you been all this week?" asked Burnett, the shop-keeper, who dealt in every description of article known to trade, from a bar of soap to a bobbin-needle, and from a saw-horse to a silk handkerchief. Of course among the articles in which he dealt, axes were numbered, and Joe Bramby was occasionally a patron. He had several acres of woodland not far from his residence, and had employed Bramby to chop off a portion of the timber. It seemed that he had not been seen in the woods for a week, and Burnett was anxious to know how the work was progressing.

"Where have you been all this week?" accordingly asked Burnett one morning when Joe made his appearance. "I haven't seen anything of you about, and they say you have not been doing anything in the woods!"

"D-d-do they?" stuttered Joe. "Well they're ab-b-bout right! I haven't been c-c-choppin' m-m-much this w-w-week—I've been all over the c-c-country on a voyage of discovery."

"Eh! after what?" asked Burnett. "Your cow strayed away?"

"N-n-no!" said Joe. "B-b-burnett, do you remember that axe you s-s-sold me a few d-d-days ago?"

"Yes," answered Burnett. "What has that to do with your voyage of discovery!"

"A g-g-good deal!" said Joe. "You'd have th-th-thought it did if you'd have seen me ch-ch-choppin' with it! I gr-gr-ground it up right sh-sh-sharp a week ago this m-m morning, and w-w-went out to the w-w-woods. I th-th-thought the axe was n-n-new, and I'd g-g-give it a f-f-fair chance, so I t-t-tried it first on a v-v-very soft p-p-pine log. What d-d-do you think h-h happened?"

"Don't know!" answered Burnett. "What the devil did happen?"

"Why, the c-c-cussedest catastrophe," said Joe —"that you ever h-h-heard of in your l-life. I struck t-t-two licks, and the th-th-third time I h-h-heard something sm-m-mash! When I l-l-looked down, there w-w-was the h-h-handle, and n-n-nothing else!"

"Well, it hadn't been in tight enough, and the axe had flown off, I suppose," said Burnett. "You ought to have wedged it in."

"Y-y-yes," said old Joe—"th-th-that would have b-b-been a good thing, if the st-t-tuff would only have st-t-tood it. I thought it h-h-had flew off the h-h-handle, and w-w-went to look for it. But j-j-jest then I s-s-seen a sq-u-u-irrel come t-t-tumbling down out of a t-t-tree, and I stopped to p-p-pick it up. What do you th-th-think had hurt it!"

"How do I know?" said Burnett, impatiently. "What had hurt it?"

"A p-p-piece of that axe!" said old Joe. "It had f-f-flew up in the t-t-top of the tree, and c-c-cut the head off of the sq-u-u-irrel as clean as a whistle."

"Whew!" said Burnett.

"Fact," said Joe. "And that w-w-wasn't the beginning! The b-b-blue-jays and r-r-robbins came t-t-tumbling d-d-down out of the t-t-trees, and the l-l-limbs f-f-fell as if there had b-b-been a h-h-hail storm. I p-p-picked up s-s-six rabbits ——"

"Oh, Lord!" said Burnett.

"Y-y-yes, m-m-more than that," Joe went on. "Several qu-qu-quail and some p-p-partridges. The p-p-pieces of that a-a-axe had c-c-cleared the under-brush off of ab-b-bout two acres, and I've been p-p-picking up the g-g-game and f-f-finding the p-p-pieces, ever since!"

The foundation of this stunner of a story of course was (and Burnett so understood it) that Joe had broken a piece of his axe the first time he used it, and had been at work somewhere else all the week.

Stephenson, another country shopkeeper, was one night trying to sell Joe a pair of pegged boots. The old man gave the article offered a fair examination, and decided not to purchase.

"Nice boots," said Stephenson.

"Y-y-yes, very nice b-b-boots," said old Joe, "b-b-but I c-c-can't afford 'em!"

"Why, they are as cheap as any they make," said Stephenson. "Only two dollars."

"Y-y-yes, only I d-d-don't k-k-keep any h-h-hired man" returned Joe.

"Hired man! what do you want of a hired man?" asked Stephenson.

"W-w-well, I should w-w-want a hired man, if I b-b-bought them b-b-boots," said Joe, his eye twisting up with even a more comical leer than usual. "The l-l-last p-p-pair of boots I h-h-had, pretty near ruined me."

"How?" asked Stephenson, who did not know old Joe quite so well as some of the other dealers.

"W-w-why," said Joe—"all the t-t-time I w-w-wore them b-b-boots, I had to t-t-take two m-m-men along with me, with h-h-hammers, one each side, to n-n-nail on the s-s soles every time I lifted my feet!"

It may be supposed that at about that period Stephenson made some discoveries as to the character of his customer, and that no more efforts were made, on that occasion, to sell him pegged boots.

Holton, a large landed proprietor, at one time employed oldJoe to clear some land for him, at a considerable distance from his (Bramby's) residence, and near Holton's. As a consequence, old Joe was obliged to eat and sleep at Holton's for a few days, instead of going home—a change which was probably no hardship.

The time was winter, and the period that before stoves had been generally introduced, and when cord-wood logs of full length were burned by the cart-load at a time, in immense old-fashicned fire-places. Holton had a large house, as well as a hospitable one, and was famed all over the country for the immense quantity of wood he consumed in his kitchen. But his house was famed for something else, not quite so agreeable—every chimney smoked so that not a room could be occupied without the door being left open. Green, a comical government contractor, who occasionally visited

Holton to buy timber, remarked that the building must have been intended for a smoke-house, and that everybody smelt like a ham for a week after coming out of it.

On the first night passed by Bramby at Holton's, the old man was sitting before the big fire in the kitchen, smoking a short black pipe, and diluting the room-full of oak and hickory smoke with a mixture of that of tobacco—when Holton came in to make some enquiries as to the chopping operations in the woods, and took a seat near him.

"Smoking, I see," said Holton. "Well, it's a good notion, for I'm sorry to say that the room does the same thing. In fact, all my rooms smoke—confound 'em!'

"Y-y-yes," answered old Joe. "There's a l-l-little of a c-c-cloud in the room. Your h-h-housekeeper had to t-t-take the b-b-bellowses a little while ago, and b-b-blow the smoke away from before b-b-black Jim's f-f-face, before she could t-t-tell w-w-whether it was h-h-him or m-m-me, so as to s-s-send him out after a b-b back load of w-w-wood."

Holton laughed, as he could not help doing, and some other remarks followed on the misfortune of having smoky-chimneys—when old Joe suggested:

"They d-d-don't all know so m-m-much about m-m-managing smoky ch-ch-chimneys as I do, Squire, or they could c-c-cure 'em!"

"Ah?" said Holton, with interest. "Did you ever see a smoky chimney cured?" It is scarcely necessary to say that this was before the day of patent chimney-pots and ventilators, or Holton would not have been likely to ask such a question.

"Seen a sm-m-oky chimney cured?" said old Joe. "I should th-th-think I h-h-had. I had the w w-worst one in Seaboard c-c-county, once, and I c-c-cured it a little t-t-too much!"

"How was that?" asked Holton, who knew his customer well, and wanted no better sport than to draw him out.

"Why, you s-s-see," said Bramby, settling himself back in the chair and taking a long whiff at his pipe—"you s-s-see I b-b-built a little h-h-house out y-y-yonder at Wolf H-h-hollow, t-t-ten or t-t-twelve years ago. Joe B-b-bush, the f-f-fellow that b-b-built the chimneys, kept b-b-blind drunk three qu-u-arters of the time, and c-c-crazy drunk the other. I t-t-told him that I th-th-thought he w-w-would have something w-w-wrong, b-b-but he stuck t-t-to it, and f-f-finished the h-h-house. Well, we m-m-moved in, and b-b-built a fire n-n-next m-m-morning to boil the t-t-tea-kettle. A-a-all the smoke c-c-came out through the r-r-room, and went out of the w-w-windows. N-n-not a devilish b-b-bit went up the f-f-flues. We t-t-tried it for two or three d-d-days, and it g-g-got worse and worse. B-b-bye and bye it c-c-come on to r-r-rain, and the rain b-b-begun to come d-d-down the chimney. It p-p-put the fire out in a m-m-minute, and d-d-directly it c-c-come down by the p-p-pailfull. We h-h-had to get the b-b-baby off the f-f-floor as soon as we c-c-could, or it w-w-would have been drownded. In f-f-fifteen minutes the w-w-water stood knee-deep on the f-f-floor. Then I w-w-went out and t-t-took a look. It d-d-didn't rain h-h-half so hard outside, and I p-p-pretty soon s-s-seen what was the m-m-matter. The d-d-drunken cuss had p-p-put the ch-ch-chimney wrong end up, and it d-d-drawed downwards! It g-g-gathered all the r-r-rain within a h-h-hundred yards, and p-p-poured it down by the b-b-bucketfull."

"Well, that was unfortunate," laughed Holton. "But what in the world did you do with the house? Surely you never cured that chimney?"

"D-d-didn't I, though!" answered old Joe. "Yes, I d-d-did!"

"How?" asked Holton.

"T-t-turned it the t-t-tother end up," said the incorrigible, "and then y-y-you ought to have s-s-seen how it drawed! That w-w-was the way I c-c-cured it too much!"

"Drew too hard?" asked Holton.

"W-w-well, Squire, you may j-j-judge for yourself," said old Joe. "P-p-pretty soon after we g-g-got the ch-ch-chimney d-d-done the other end up, I m-m-missed one of the ch-ch-chairs out of the r-r-room, and d-d-directly I s-s-seen another of 'em s-s-scooting along t-t-towards the fire-place. N-n-next the t-t-table went, and I s-s-seen the b-b-back-log going up. Then I g-g-grabbed the old w-w-woman under one arm and the b-b-baby under t-t-tother, and started; b-b-but just as I g-g-got to the d-d-door I seen the cat going across the f-f-floor, b-b-backwards, h-h-holding on with her claws to the c-c-carpet, and yelling awfully. It w-w-wasn't no use —I j-j-just seen her g-g-going over the t-t-top of the ch-ch-chimney, and that was the l-l-last of her!"

"Well, what did you do 'then?" asked Holton. "Of course you could'nt live in such a house!"

"C-c-couldn't I, though!" answered old Joe. "But I d-d-did! I p-p-put a p-p-poultice on the j-j-jamb of the fire-place, and that d-d-drawed the tother w-w-way, so that we h-h-had no more trouble."

This was always regarded, in the neighborhood, as the crowning achievement of old Joe Bramby. Only one more instance, and that a brief one, need be given, as a taste of his quality.

Bramby was pricing some umbrellas at a shop on Greenwich street, in this city, during one of his few visits to the metropolis. The salesman was expati ating on the excellence of the article, when Joe sent him to the right-about with the inquiry:

"H-h-how much will it l-l-leak?"

"Why, not at all?" indignantly said the salesman.

"C-c-cause I don't like 'em to l-l-leak too much," said Bramby. "They're d-d-dangerous!"

"How?" asked the astonished clerk.

"I b-b-bought one n-n-not long ago," gravely proceeded the old romancer, "and w-w-went out in the r-r-rain w-w-with it. I s-s-soon found that it was r-r-raining a cussed sight h-h-harder under the u-u-umbrella than it was outside, and if I h-h-hadn't folded it up and p-put it under my arm as qu-u-uick as I c-c-could, it would have d-d-drowned me!"

III.

SYMPATHY AND SMALL CHANGE.

My friend Tom Brower went over to Hoboken one day last summer, just when the small financial troubles first began to come fairly upon the country. A lady friend of his from a distant town was visiting the city, and he was under some sort of engagement to show her the lions. Among the lions she had not seen, was Hoboken. She had never seen the Otto Cottage, whereat the band plays and the Teutonic damsels dance, while the swains who are not dancing with them discuss "zwei lager." She had never seen Fox Hill and the cricket-ground—never gazed upon the Elysian Fields, where the clubs play ball, and the yachts make their start on the morning of the great annual regatta of the silver tea-pot. She had never stood on the esplanade near Sybil's Cave and looked up the river to the Palisades, the steamboats and the sloops going (not the Palisades) in that direction.

So Tom and his lady went to Hoboken, leaving by the steamer from the foot of Barclay street at five o'clock, P. M. They strolled to Fox Hill and the Elysian Fields, taking a look in at the Cottage as they went by. They admired the beauties of Nature everywhere, and the beauties of art about Castle Point particularly. They looked up the river and down the river, and heard the Armenia's calliope playing "Life Let us Cherish" and several other things, as she came down past the city on her way from Albany. They peeped in at the Sybil's Cave, and——

Here they got hungry, as was not unnatural after a long walk and an early lunch. Thereupon they sat down on one of the benches, by one of the tables in the cool *al fresco* refectory in front of the Sybil's Cave, and ordered a lunch and a couple of cooling drinks, *with* straws. Tom's bill, when he came to pay it, was only forty cents, which was reasonable enough, only that on fumbling in his pockets he found that he had only five cents in change! Change was scarce (this was before the postage-stamp currency made it a drug) and ruled at fifteen per cent. premium in Wall street. But Tom had nothing else to do than to tender a bill, which he did —tendered it very tenderly indeed, for fear the mild Teuton of the refectory should scold. The Teuton *did* scold a little, and demanded change, which Tom declared himself unable to supply. Thereupon the Teuton, under the pressure of necessity, and with many observations showing how generous he was, took the one dollar bill and returned Tom two quarters and a ten cent piece in sterling. Tom put the change somewhat hurriedly into his pocket, and lugged his lady friend away under a sort of dim consciousness that he had been guilty of imposing upon good nature by presuming to take an evening lunch at the *al fresco* refectory in front of Sybil's Cave, without having the specie to liquidate the bill.

Then Tom and his lady friend strolled leisurely down the river, towards the ferry.

When Tom and his lady friend reached the ferry, and he attempted to pay their ferriage over by the thoroughly seasoned (about forty seasons) and altogether reliable steamer Newark, to the foot of Canal street—

He found that his generous and self-sacrificing friend at the *al fresco* refectory in front of the Sybil's Cave, had stuck him with one pewter quarter and one lead ten cent piece.

Whereupon he altered his mind considerably as to the kind spirit which had been displayed, and his lady friend laughed in the most consoling manner.

It was dusk when Tom and his lady friend reached Broadway at Canal street, and as they were going to Wallack's Theatre and the hour was late, they rode up.

The stage-driver felt insulted at the proffer of a bill, and demanded change. Tom felt hurt at the demand, alleging that he had none, and appealing to the passengers in proof that he was ill-used. When he had sufficiently excited the sympathy of the passengers, and got the driver too much flustered to make any very close examination of what he got *instead* of a bill—Tom suddenly discovered, by searching his pockets, that he *had* a ten cent piece and two pennies, and passed them up through the hole. The driver stuck them into the box with a chuckle, which said very plainly: "Oho, Mr. Passenger! you did not get a bill on me, that time!" which was very true, but the ten cents—ahem!

Tom and his lady friend went to Wallack's to see Billy Florence and his wife in "Temptation" and "Fra Diavolo." During one of the intermissions Tom went down into the saloon, having a thirsty throat, no doubt induced by the buffalo-tongue he had eaten at lunch. Just as he approached the counter, one of the shyster fraternity was swallowing a glass of beer, price six cents, and tendering a dollar bill in payment. Of course the bar-keeper was indignant, and asked the shyster sharply whether he had no change. The shyster said that he had not, and the bar-keeper, with a look of intense disgust upon his face, told him to " take his bill and clear out!"

Tom sympathetically approached the bar-keeper, asked him whether there were many of those fellows who were mean enough to take advantage of the scarcity of change to tender bills in payment for a purchase of six cents when specie commanded a premium of fifteen, and bitterly denounced the conduct of any man who could commit such an outrage on the integrity of retail mercantile transactions.

The bar-keeper looked grateful for the sympathy, and said to himself: "There is a man who has the true principles of integrity at heart! He would not be caught doing such a thing!"

Of course not!

Under the fog he had raised by his sympathy, Tom succeeded in passing the pewter quarter on the bar-keeper for a julep, and effected his retreat in good order.

So much for small change, and so much for sympathy, as Sir Peter Teazle might have told us shortly after his great interview with Joseph Surface.

IV.

TEN DOLLARS' WORTH OF DOG.

An occurrence of a few months ago leads me to doubt whether all the dog abstractions are conducted by ragged boys and scoundrelly "dog-fanciers." Pointers may therefore sometimes point a moral, setters be set turning the wheel of popular merriment, bull-dogs be made responsible for blunders, and even a worthless cur be the means of a comical occurrence. The parties in this dog-operation are well known to most men of business on the street; but the price I must pay for the privilege of being allowed to retail the story at all (no canine pun intended)—is of course a total concealment of the names involved.

I may call my principal actor Tom Ernest, from the double reason that it is not by any means his name, and that the surname has a spice of the German, to which class of adopted citizens, either himself or through his parentage, my friend Tom belongs. He is a good-looking fellow of thirty, partner in a commercial house not a hundred miles from the post-office—a jolly good fellow in every particular—and the least trifle in the world gay, though he has been for a few years married to a charming wife who should have cured him of any rapid predilections. He lives in very comfortable quarters in a street not very far from Union Square; and his family circle is added to, both in numbers and happiness, by the presence of a very charming sister-in-law, who is quite as full of mischief as the laws of society will possibly allow.

I met Ernest coming out of a well-known restaurant and lunch-room, not far from his place of business, at the time referred to. His face was stretched to nearly twice its usual width, and he was indulging in the luxury of an unmistakeable chuckle which shook him to the ends of his boots. I am fond of chuckles, when I know what they are about and do not find them confined to the capacity of one. So I laid violent hands upon Tom, and partially shook out of him the secret of his merriment, albeit he informed me that he had just promised "never to say a word about it as long as he lived." Dog was, as might have been expected, at the bottom of the affair.

It appears that Tom, his wife, and the mischievous sister-in-law before mentioned, had been making an evening call at the house of a merchant doing business in the same street with Ernest—the house being only a few blocks away from his own domicil. The merchant, who may for the present rejoice in the rare appellation of Jones, goes over to the country in the bird-season, and is particularly choice in the breed of some setters and pointers which he keeps in cosy kennels in the back yard. He is reported to have paid fabulous prices for some of these peculiar animals, and generally supposed—money apart—to have nearly as ardent an affection for his canine breed as he holds for his family—the latter remark not being at all intended to disparage his domestic attachments.

Tom and the ladies with him were going to walk home, and they had already made their adieux, descended the front steps and had the door shut behind them—when a very fine pointer that Tom knew was worth one or two hundreds in his friend's estimation—emerged from the front area. He had not been duly incarcerated in his kennel for the night, through some inadvertence; and when the servant-girl closed the basement door for the night, our pointer had been left out in the area, subject to all the accidents and escapes incident to the canine fraternity. Hearing the sound of voices, he had probably come up the area steps to ask in dog-language that he might be returned to his old quarters, as the traditional old prisoner of the Bastile did after his few hours' indulgence in the free sunshine.

Tom Ernest, who loves dogs, patted the pointer on the head, said "nice dog" as usual, and was about going up the steps again to ring and inform the family of the position of the truant—when the merry sister-in-law laid her hand suddenly on his arm.

"Stop, Tom! did you ever steal anything?"

"Humph! rather a hard question to ask of a merchant!" answered Tom, surprised. "Why?"

"Couldn't you steal that dog?" asked the young mischief, as innocently as if she had been suggesting the most orderly proceeding in the world.

"What do you mean?" asked Tom.

"Mean? why," answered the tempter—"steal the dog—hook him, if you like the word any better. Coax him along home with us, or may be you could carry him. Shut him up somewhere, in the pot-closet or the coal-cellar, and keep him snug. See what fun there would be in old Jones looking for him all over town!"

"Humph! eh? well, the idea isn't so bad!" said Ernest.

"Shame, Tom! to think of such a thing!" said the prudent and practical wife.

"Shame? I don't see the shame," said the mischievous sister-in-law, with a pout that might have been seen if the night had been a little less dusky. "Only a joke, and serve old Jones right! What business has he to keep dogs stuck away in his back-yard, if he don't want somebody to steal them?"

"Well, I am just going to take that dog along!" said Tom, to whose vision the joke had now grown into most tempting proportions. "Just keep still, and see that none of them open the door or peep through the blinds. The dog knows me, and I think he will come along without much difficulty. Here, Spot! poor fellow!"

The pointer seemed pleased with the attention, but when the experiment was tried of inducing him to follow, he hung back, as if he had not quite made up his mind as to the act of secession. Thereupon Tom would probably have abandoned the project, but that the incarnate female mischief had a long scarf off her neck in a moment, and deposited it in his hands, with a hint that "there was something to lead him with."

The pointer did not make serious objections to the application of the scarf, and in a moment he was safely tethered and following the party—Tom with some idea that he might be arrested for dog-stealing, his wife heartily ashamed of him for the first time in her life, and the sister-in-law nearly choking with laughter at intervals, in view of the ridiculous character of the whole affair, and the anticipation of Jones' grief and astonishment at the loss of his canine treasure.

Half an hour afterwards the captive was duly installed in the coal vault, as the tempter had suggested—amply provided with clean straw and supplied with food enough to have driven him into a dyspepsia if he had only consumed it. There, faithfully waited upon by the fair cause of his abduction, who would not have permitted him to suffer under any consideration—the pointer passed the next sixty hours, till the second act of the canine drama had transpired.

The *Herald* was duly examined the next morning at the breakfast-table at Ernest's, but without result. The abduction had not been discovered the night before in time to secure the publication. That day Tom happened in at the place of business of Jones. He found him in immense tribulation at the loss, and declaring that "Spot was the best pointer he had. He would not have looked at a hundred dollars for him! He had no doubt some young scoundrel had stolen him, and very likely some of the servant girls had helped in the robbery and shared the profit!" Tom did not attempt to combat the idea, but expressed his deep regret, and duly aided Jones in objurating the thief who could thus sever the bonds between a hundred-dollar pointer and his attached master. Having remained nearly as long as he felt that he could ensure his mouth against being detected in a broad grin, he went back to his own place of business.

The examination of the *Herald* next morning, was more satisfactory. The sister-in-law pounced upon the precious paragraph, as a bird might be supposed to do upon a very dainty vermiculous morsel. It read as follows:—

LOST.—ON TUESDAY NIGHT LAST, FROM THE RESIDENCE of his owner, No. —, —— street, a valuable Pointer Dog. [Here followed the description.] Ten Dollars Reward will be paid for his return to the office of Bradford & Jones, No. —, —— street, and no questions will be asked.

"There it is—all right—just as I told you it would be!" said the originator of the frolic, when she had done reading the advertisement. "Now, you see, if you only send him back by somebody that Jones does not know, you would be ten dollars ahead."

"Why, how could you think of such a thing, sister?" said Tom's wife. "Surely, Mr. Ernest, you would not carry the joke so far as that!"

"That would be carrying the joke quite as far as we carried the dog—eh, wife?" laughed Tom. "Running it into the ground—just as we ran him into it—in the coal-vault!"

"But you don't mean to spoil a good joke by only carrying it out half-way, do you?" said the temptation. "Haven't you some person about the store—"

"Yes, I have it!" said Tom. "There is Mike, our porter; I will send him. I don't think Jones knows him from Adam. You both know him, and when Mike comes for the dog, let him take him. One might as well be hung for an old sheep as a lamb, you know; and how the deuce am I going to get the dog back to Jones unless I adopt some plan of the kind?"

"Just so!" said the tormentor; and Tom's wife, though she may mentally have demurred, said nothing more. Before Tom left the house that morning for his business, the rest of the programme was arranged.

Within two hours afterward, Mike, the Irish porter, had received his instructions. He was to go to the house—get the dog—take him to Bradford & Jones' office, with a copy of the *Herald*—draw the money and report again to Tom—making no explanations, and leaving the impression on the mind of Jones that he was some idle fellow who was probably in the habit of picking up anything that might be left lying around loose. To this end he was provided with a very bad coat and a smashed hat, and so equipped he set out on his mission.

All worked well. The pointer was duly released from his place of "temporary retirement," decorated with a rope, and led down to the store of Bradford & Jones, where he was received with a general chorus of gratification by all the employees (who probably did not care a snap for the dog, but took that mode of conciliating one of *the partners*), —and with enthusiastic rejoicings by the lately-bereaved dog-proprietor himself. He examined his pet pointer at all points—as Mike reported on his return—felt his ribs to see whether he had fallen away in flesh during his absence—patted him as if he had been a favorite child receiving the paternal blessing—and acted generally as if he would have hugged his canine treasure outright but for the presence of others.

Mike came back, reported progress, and paid over the ten dollars to Ernest, who duly stowed it away for early use. A carriage was meanwhile called for Jones, who took his recovered animal inside with himself, to guard against any more accidents, and went home at once to restore him to his kennel and receive the congratulations of his family.

The next day Ernest called upon Jones, ostensibly to make some inquiries as to the standing of a customer. His real object may be pretty easily divined. He had not to wait very long for what he had expected. Jones was so full of "dog" that he could not keep the subject long under.

"By the way, Ernest," he said, breaking in upon a subject that was very different—"I have found my dog!"

"What! is it possible!" said Tom. "Where on earth did he come from? Who brought him back?"

"I don't know," answered Jones, "and in fact I was so glad to see him that I never asked. He was an Irishman, I noticed, and shabbily dressed—that is all I know. Are you not glad? Don't you congratulate me?"

"Of course I do!" replied Tom. "Glad to hear that you have got him back, from the bottom of my heart. In fact—can you go out for a few minutes? If you can, we will drink to the good health of 'Spot,' and the hope that he may never be strayed or stolen again."

"Much obliged to you, Ernest, I am sure!" said Jones, flattered at Tom's evident interest. "I knew you would be glad to hear that I had got him back again. Wouldn't have taken a hundred dollars for that dog."

"And only cost you ten to get him back," remarked Tom—"besides that little advertisement."

So they went out to bibulate over the joyful event. Mixed liquors were ordered, and Ernest threw down a ten dollar bill. They clinked glasses in honor of the return, and "smiled" amicably and audibly. When they had set down the glasses and the change was laid on the bar, Ernest pushed it across to Jones.

"What do you mean?" asked the latter in surprise. "*You* put down the ten dollar bill, didn't you?"

"Yes," answered Tom, slowly, "but the change is yours, for all that!"

"I don't see the joke," said Jones, "though of course there must be one somewhere! How do you come to owe me ten dollars?"

"*Dog!*" said Tom Ernest, fixing his laughing eyes full on Jones.

Jones understood, without another word of explation, and was at first inclined to commit an assault and battery on Ernest, but thought better of it. But they did not separate until Tom had detailed the whole operation, with the share which his temptress had takin in inducing it; nor until Tom had solemnly promised that he would not mention any names if he ever told the story.

The last act in the drama had just occurred when I met Tom Ernest exploding with laughter as at first recorded; but somehow or other, though I have not mentioned the names here, they have leaked out, and Jones has already been obliged to add various quarters to the original expenditure of "Ten Dollars' Worth of Dog."

V.

WHY TOM BURT DIDN'T SWEAR.

Tom Burt always swore and swore awfully, except *once*. Why he failed to perform that ordinary operation on the occasion referred to, it is the duty and the mission of this hasty sketch to explain.

A considerable number of years ago in a section of country which is not of the least consequence for the purposes of this narrative, Tom followed the business of a "carter." He kept two or three teams, and carted every description of article that any one wished to have transported, from a keg of butter to a saw-log, just as the cartmen in this city transport any description of furniture or merchandize. A strong, stout, athletic fellow was Tom Burt—able to load with his single strength what would puzzle half a dozen others, and therefore always the more in demand. But strong as were his arms and back, he had a still more athletic *tongue*. He could probably out-swear any man within the circle of a hundred miles around him; and when fairly aroused by some impertinence addressed to himself, or by a succession of untoward circumstances occurring in business—it was always remarked by those in his neighborhood that the sky assumed a sickly green color, and that a strong perfume of sulphur and æsofedita filled the atmosphere. It finally became a common remark with reference to any one who swore loosely and indiscriminately, that he "ripped and tore almost as bad as Tom Burt."

A neighbor of Burt's was one season cutting off the wood on a row of hedge-land overlooking a long sweep of meadow, and at the foot of a range of steep, precipitous hills. Among the trees were found several massive old oaks, the butt-cuts of which made immense, unwieldy saw-logs, very valuable as timber but terribly difficult to handle. The difficulty was added to by the fact that there was no road over the meadow, and that the logs must be got to the saw-mill by laboriously dragging them up the hill-sides to the level of the road above.

To get some of the heaviest of these up, Tom Burt, with heavy timber-wagons and strong horses, was employed. With half a dozen extra men to assist in loading, and six horses harnessed to one of his strongest wagons, Burt commenced the task. It was not by any means a pleasant one, and strained backs, smashed fingers, and swearing were the order of the day as some of the smaller logs were loaded and dragged up the hill. Burt was peculiarly fresh and lively in his cursing, and when anything occurred to vex him for a moment, he let off such a volley that day, that even the rough fellows he had employed, shuddered as if they believed the angry sky was coming down on their heads.

Finally the giant of the group was tackled. With almost superhuman labor it was loaded on the wagon, then chocked and chained so as to be safe for its upward ride. The big horses groaned and the stout wagon creaked, as they labored zig-zag up the precipitous hill, and occasionally it was necessary to apply pries and the shoulders of the men to the wheels, to prevent stopping and going backward at some sharper acclivity. Up and up, until they were very nearly at the top, when at a quick short jerk the bolt gave way that secured the tongue of the wagon to the hounds, the wagon went suddenly backwards with its fearful load, took a shear in the road, went over and was crushed to pieces; and the big log, released from its bonds, went over, and over and over again, crashing through the underbrush and ploughing through the turf, thundering along to the very bottom of the hill where it leaped the hedge to the edge of the meadow and landed in a ditch, from which there were scarcely men and teams enough in the country to extricate it.

Every eye of the men employed turned upon Tom Burt, and every ear prepared for such a volley of profanity as had not before been heard since the English army did such tall swearing in Flanders. Burt stood there, calm and serene, his arms folded, his eye scanning the whole catastrophe, but not a word proceeding from his lips. Dead silence with himself and his assistants, lasting for several moments. There seemed to be a general feeling that whatever was to be done, Burt must do, and yet Burt did nothing.

At length Joe Brown, Burt's second in command and only his second in profanity, found it impossible any longer to restrain his astonishment.

"Tom Burt!" he said, "why the d—l don't you swear?"

"Swear!" said Burt, his concentrated rage hissing through his teeth, but no oath following. "Swear! Well, boys, I never wanted to swear so bad in my life, but I can't! I thought I could rip a little; and I have more than once cussed the bark off a big hickory, and made a hen-hawk drop right out of the air as if he had been shot, when I fired one of them big oaths at him? But that 'are log, smashing up that 'are wagon, rollin' down the hill and goin' kerslump into a bog that it can never be got out of till the general resurrection—that takes me! I give up! Swearin' ain't no use. If I was to cuss till sundown I couldn't do justice to it, so don't ask me!"

It is needless to say that Joe Brown and all the rest held Tom excusable for that occasion, and for that occasion *only*. I am not aware that Tom ever was known to fail afterwards, as he certainly had never failed before.

VI.

BILLY RADFORD'S LOST PUP.

THERE stands out clearly and prominently before my mind's eye, at this moment, a canine of tender years belonging to one Billy Radford—the loss of that valuable animal—the exertions made by Mr. Radford, aforesaid, to secure the return of his missing pet—the number of times that pet (or some other) was brought back to him—with other entertaining particulars belonging to the whole transaction.

Radford was a dapper clerk in one of those nondescript conglomerations of incongruous merchandize y'clept a country store—one of those places in which silks and soap, calicoes and codfish, mittens and medicines, are dispensed to a variety of customers quite as great as the variety of the goods on sale. One of those places in which a country fine lady, come to do her "shopping" (she can do it, by the way, quite as efficiently, heartlessly and injuriously, as if she had been educated on Chesnut street, or spent half her life and all her husband's money, practising on Broadway)—where the country fine lady, I say, looking for silks, flannels or ribbons, is jostled by the dirty boy who has been sent in a hurry to replace a defunct corn-hoe,—or by a female Ethiopian of moderate pretensions, no bonnet and a very dirty gown, anxious after a bar of soap or two pounds of sugar.

Radford, as I have said, filled the position of clerk or counter-jumper in such an establishment, so near to the place where I was at that time located, in a country village within sight of the smoke of the great city, that I had a reasonably close acquaintance with the details of his daily life, and spent very much of my time assisting him in his arduous labors of sitting on the counter in the absence of customers, smoking very bad cigars when the proprietor happened to be temporarily missing, and playing chequers in the intervals of more profitable employment.

Some malevolent fate ordered it, one summer, that Billy should become the proprietor of a dog. Not a very large dog, certainly, nor yet a very costly dog; but large enough for all practical purposes, and which eventually cost him enough to have been reckoned a dear acquisition. Holt, a small farmer who paid much more attention to the dog and gun than to the acres which should have made him independent, and who lived half a mile across the valley, was somewhat noted as a breeder of dogs. Among his variety he had succeeded in producing a cross between the common yellow hound and the English spotted coach dog, that was really very handsome and of no possible use in the world. The desire to procure slips of this remarkable breed ran high one summer; and by using very fine words with Holt, and depositing in his itching palm perhaps five dollars of current coin, Radford, who no more wanted a dog than the same dog would have wanted a supplementary head on the other end,—succeeded in procuring one of them—a pup of a few months old, tall, slight of limb, glossy of coat, and daintily spotted—a very nice thing to look at, if one could only have known what to do with it, and if it had been no trouble.

Billy at the time took his meals at the house of his employer, at a little distance, and slept in a part of the store-building; so that he really made his home at his place of business. Of course his canine acquisition must be provided quarters at this place; and the dapper clerk put on overalls, soiled his hands and blistered his fingers, in the construction of a kennel on the lot adjoining the building, where his pet, though confined within bounds by the moderate length of his chain, would enjoy all the other comforts of dog-hood. Thither Billy transported him tit-bits from his own dinner, and choice morsels from the uncooked meats that lay in the barrels of the grocery department. There, too, he watered him as if he had been a favorite flower. For some days after the acquisition, it is safe to say that Billy visited the kennel twenty times a day, for a romp with his four-footed friend, and spent half the remaining time somewhat to the disadvantage of business, in peering lovingly out of a favorable window that overlooked the location of his treasure.

One morning, the night before which had been an exquisite moonlight, there was not precisely mounting in hot haste, on the part of Billy Radford, but flying around half dressed and in most remarkable agitation. Taking a preliminary glance out of the window of the chamber as he descended, lo and behold a sad spectacle met his gaze! The end of a broken chain was visible, extending out for a couple of feet from the door of the kennel. Billy realized all his misfortune at once. His "purp" was gone—his beautiful "purp" from which a "dorg" of magnificent dimensions had been expected to grow. Billy took about three steps down stairs, two more brought him out to the kennel—all his worst fears were but too truly accomplished. The pup was among those sad things upon which the memory might rest, but the sight of which was evermore denied to the living eyes. Talk about "banquet halls deserted," and the melancholy condition of the duck-ponds and sidewalks at "Sweet Auburn"—all these could have been nothing to the desolate appearance of the deserted kennel. Billy seemed to see the pup yet at the end of the chain, as his eyes filled with tears; and he more than half thought that he could hear his delicious howl, with which for a few nights he had kept all the neighbors and Billy himself awake,—echoing through the halls of memory. He examined the chain; it had not been cut off, but broken; the pup had not then, probably, been stolen, but must have broken his chain during the night, and escaped from the house that had been so lovingly prepared for him; from the hand that had so fed—and watered—him.

Billy went back to the store a young man of altered feelings—not to say of a crushed spirit. His hair had not suddenly whitened, neither had there grown a sudden stoop in his back, indicating premature age. But his elasticity of spirit was gone. He saw the vanity and evanescence of human possessions. When a small boy came after a quart of molasses, he asked him instead how much "dog;" and when he was required to make out a bill for some dry goods purchased by a lady for her family, he began it—"Mrs. ——, to W. Radford, Dr., to one spotted pup." Billy had, in fact, "pup on the brain."

This sad state of affairs could not last. Action was necessary, or the mental consequences might be serious. Of course he asked every one who came in whether they had seen his dog, and was always answered in the negative. Then his desolate spirit found relief in advertising, as so many other people have erewhile found it in other walks of literature.

No newspaper was within easy reach, nor was there a printing-office in the village. But the resource of the pen and of the marking-brush with which he marked bundles, was yet open to him. He went diligently to work, and the result that followed was comprised in six sheets of white writing paper, reading as follows, and the heading of each done with the marking-brush, while the balance was filled up with the pen in coarse-hand:

"DOG LOST.

"STRAYED OR STOLEN!!

"The subscriber has lost a spotted pup, four months old, and big for his age. Said pup is very handsome, and is called "Jack." He looks a little like a hound, but is spotted all over with nice spots. Said pup was taken away or broke his chain on Thursday night, back of Mr. ——'s store, at ——. If any body will bring back the said pup in good order, to the said store, without cutting off his ears or tail, or spoiling his spots, he will receive a liberal reward and the thanks of the owner.

"WILLIAM RADFORD.

"P. S.—Nobody needn't be afraid of the said pup, for he doesn't bite at all. He can be took up, harmless as a child. W. R."

These notices were at once duly posted, by order of the proper authorities. One was stuck up by Billy himself on one of the piazza posts of the store, and another on a board fence in the immediate neighborhood. A third was sent by a customer who happened to stop with his wagon, to be posted at a tavern two miles off. The remainder were entrusted to a small boy belonging to one of the neighboring families, with a hammer and some lath-nails, and his pockets filled with crackers and raisins as a compensation for performing the duty—to be nailed on a certain tree at a neighboring cross-roads, and disposed in two other public situations. Then, not having, perhaps, commanded success, but having taken those steps which seemed to deserve it—it may be supposed Radford was easier in his mind, and he transacted the business of the day with less of blunders—such as weighing out Scotch snuff when called on for cassimere, or supplying a lady with a chopping-axe instead of an ounce of nutmegs—than might have been the case had he omitted the hand-bills. We may fancy, too, that he retired to rest with more hope of sleep than might have been indulged in the first hours of his bereavement.

But that sleep was broken. Among the materials for supplying the general wants of the neighborhood, afforded by the store, drugs and medicines were to be reckoned—from a patent pill that would cure all the ills that flesh is heir to, by merely smelling of the box—down through all the varieties of ordinary aperients and opiates, to an ointment which would cause the hair to grow on the back of a pine board. In order to prevent the possibility of some respected citizen dying quietly at midnight without being able to procure the necessary medicine to help him off—a night-bell had been arranged at the door of the store, communicating with Radford's chamber, so that a pull upon the handle at the door would tingle a bell within a foot of the ear of the sleeping clerk.

At about midnight came a pull. Tingle—lingle! went the bell. Radford jumped out of bed as if he had been shot out by a catapult. Here was his dog, now! Somebody had read the notice—picked up the animal, and could not wait until morning to return him and claim the "liberal reward." At once he flung up the window—through which he could be heard, though not seen, the roof of the piazza hiding the person below.

"Have you got him?" he called out.

"Yes, but how the devil did you know?" was the response, in a gruff tone. "Come, hurry down!"

"Where was he?" responded Billy, still through the window.

"Down by the creek," was the reply. "Somebody had hit him on the head, and he was as stiff as a poker when we found him."

"Good heavens!" cried Radford. "Poor Jack! is he dead, then?" elevating his voice so that his interlocutor could hear the question.

"Dead, no! He's coming to, gradually, but he must have some morphine at once. They had to cut his boots off his feet, they were swelled so. But why in thunder don't you hurry down?"

"Cut off his feet!—good Lord!" cried poor Radford, who had not caught all the words of the other. "Cut off his feet? why what will he be good for? Yes, yes, I'm coming down as soon as I get dressed. Poor Jack! oh, my pretty pup!"

Two or three minutes elapsed, and then Radford opened the front door. There stood Joe Manson, a workman from the lime-kilns. But he seemed to have no dog with him.

"Where is he? why don't you bring him in?" asked Radford, impetuously, as he looked in vain for the dog.

"Come, Bill Radford, you'd better go to bed again and sleep off that drunk!" said Hanson. "Where should he be, but in his bed, and how could *I* bring him here?"

"In bed?—put him in bed and cut off his legs?" added Radford—"why what *do* you mean?"

"Can't stand talking here all night," said Hanson. "Come, get the morphine if you're going to. Didn't say that they had cut off his legs, only the *boots* off his legs."

"Boots? why where the deuce did he get *boots* from?" queried Radford, relieved, however, by the supposed intelligence that his pet had not lost his legs. "Had some of the boys been playing tricks on him and then knocked him on the head?"

"Don't know!" answered Hanson. "All we know is, that he was at Loper's tavern along in the evening, and had been drinking a little. When they found him, his watch was gone——"

"Joe Hanson, what *are* you talking about?" broke out poor Billy. "A dog that has been drinking and lost his watch!"

"No," said Hanson, "it's you that has been drinking. I was talking about Sam Hays, that we picked up down the creek to-night, near dead. What the d—l was *you* talking about?"

"Hem," said Radford—"don't know exactly. Perhaps I must have been a little asleep yet. Said you wanted morphine, eh? Haven't seen anything of a nice spotted hound pup, around anywhere, have you?"

"No, cuss your pup!" roughly answered Hanson. "Bill Radford, you have kept me half an hour, and Hays may die before I get back, just for want of the medicine! Come, stir yourself!"

Poor Billy lit his lamp, weighed out the medicine, which may have been morphine, or *cam*-phene for anything that I know to the contrary, or for anything that he probably knew at the time,—and Hanson departed.

"Thought he was talking about my pup!" mused

Radford as he once more crept back to bed. "Well, I'm glad it wasn't him, if he had been used in any such way as that!" and he went once more to his broken slumbers, in which he dreamed that Jack made his appearance with a bloody head, two of his legs cut off and the other two cased in waterman's boots, and with a watch of the dimensions of a brass kettle tied to his tail. No farther interruption that night, and he arose in the morning to mourn his loss by daylight.

But the pup soon arrived, in another shape. Radford had some lady customers during the morning —among others two at one time, of whom one was the daughter of a neighboring farmer, towards whom Billy had a peculiar warming of the heart which might afterwards have grown to a matrimonial flame. She was a saucy little minx, as well as a pretty one; and when she came to buy calicoes, laces or ribbons, and to trade away a pot of butter or a few dozens of eggs, the transaction always occupied a considerable time, if the proprietor happened to be absent,—through the manœuvring of Billy and the coquettish willingness of Lucy to trade off one labial kiss for a dozen candy ones, or fill her pockets with oranges and almonds at a corresponding consideration.

On the morning in question Lucy and a neighbor girl were in the store, and Radford was doing the amiable, after having—as is almost unnecessary to say—communicated the loss of his pup and expatiated on the beauty thereof,—when a small specimen of male darkeyhood, about ten years old and three feet high, entered the front door, dragging along an animal of the dog species. The little nigger was blacker than the dark cellar into which the sable necromancer went at night to look for his black cat; and his eyes and his teeth, which occupied more than half his face, were of such snowy whiteness that they seemed to glitter, starlike, in the black mass of their surroundings. Sartorially, he was a mass of patched rags, with an unfortunate rent in the patches of his nether habiliments, through which pieces of a shirt that had once been white presented themselves. But if the little darkey was an object, what was the animal accompanying him? Imagine a dog with the body of a bull-dog; the six-inches-long legs of a whiffet; the hair of a wiry cur, standing up on end as if he had been rough-dried and nobody had had time to iron him; two inches of stumpy tail that stood bolt upright like a flag-staff; a head large enough for a moderate-sized lion, with bobbed ears, flabby hanging jaws, a red mouth and bleared red eyes; then impart a color suggestive of having taken his nightly slumber in an ash-heap—and a fair idea may be conceived of the appearance presented by the animal brought to Radford for inspection. No married lady could have looked upon it without serious peril to herself and family. It had the effect of freezing Radford temporarily to stone, and of sending Lucy doubled up across the counter in a paroxysm of laughter which threatened her life.

"He! he! got your pup, Masser Radford!" said the juvenile incarnation of blackness.

"*That* my dog!" cried Radford, breaking momentarily from the spell which bound him.

"Yes, that is your dog!" laughed Lucy, breaking into another fit of irrepressible merriment. "You said he was a beauty, and he is! only look at him!"

"That's not my dog! the d—l!" roared Radford, coloring and paling by turns.

"Oh yes, sartin—must be your dog, Masser Radford," said the little wretch. "Jim Burns told me it was, and said he'd seen some kind of writin' about it. Must be your dog, Masser Radford, sartin!"

"I tell you it is *not*," said Billy, savagely. "You'd better get out of the store with that ugly cuss, or I'll break your black head!"

"Pshaw! don't!" said Lucy, with a great affectation of sobriety. "Now, Billy, own up like a man! If the dog isn't so good-looking as you pretended, don't scold the little darkey and back out from what you promised to pay."

"Thunder and lightning!" cried Radford, now fairly beside himself with vexation, "I tell you that it *isn't* my pup! Do you think that I'd have such a looking thing as *that* about me?"

"Well, he *isn't* pretty!" laughed Lucy, "but I guess he must be yours, Billy. Come, take him like a man, off the poor little fellow's hands, and give him what you owe him."

"Yes, give me what you owe me, Masser Radford?" whined the little nigger, putting his knuckles in his eyes, and either crying or affecting to cry, while Radford on one side and the blear-eyed dog on the other, looked particularly dangerous and wolfish.

"Get out, I tell you! off with you before I break your head!" and Radford made a demonstration to spring at negro and dog with a wooden cloth-roller, whereupon the small imp of darkness took to his heels, now bellowing in earnest, and dropping the string by which he had led the dog. The latter immediately took refuge behind a row of barrels, from between which his head looked out, the teeth grinning savagely and his position defended by a series of barks and growls which nearly drove the poor clerk distracted.

Away went the cloth-roller at the dog, followed by an application of hoe-handle, which happened to be the next thing that fell into the hands of poor badgered Billy. The dog finally took flight out of the store and up the road, while the little negro stood bellowing outside, his fists stuck into his eyes, and likely to attract more attention from passers-by than might be agreeable. The result of which was, that at Lucy's suggestion the poor little black morsel was called in, a bright quarter put in his hand, and his pockets stuffed full of peanuts—at which he went away not only satisfied, but rejoicing, and Billy Radford was rid of this ban-dog incubus.

But visitation number three was not long in coming, though fortunately it did not arrive until Lucy had gone away, or the second attack of risibility might really have cost her life. Two hours after dinner, and when Radford was alone in the store, entered a stalwart Hibernian, whose thick and muddy boots proclaimed him to be by profession a digger of ditches. He, too, had a dog, dragged in by a small rope which had probably been his wife's clothes-line. And in the *quantity* of dog, there was nearly as much difference between the new-comer and the one that had preceded it, as there was between the little nigger and the big Irishman.

The dog was evidently a mixture of the bull-dog of the fiercest description, and the mastiff. He was large-boned and heavy legged, with the protruding jaw of the prize-fighter and the retreating forehead of the idiot. He was piebald white, brindle and black in color, and over one of the eyes of his partially white face was a daub of black that exactly suggested the damaged optic of his prototype the pugilist. He was lame of one foot, and had an ominous bloody strip down one side, as if from a recent fight, but evidently had not all the fight taken out of him, for his heavy tail wagged treacherously, his white teeth showed through the red muzzle, and he kept up a constant low growl that suggested throttling somebody or something. His keeper was ill-favored and red-whiskered, and had a sapling cudgel in his hand that might have been employed in pounding the ugly brute into submission, and might be intended to perform the same operation on the person visited.

"Is it here fwhere you want the dog?" asked the pleasant-looking visitor.

"I lost a dog, night before last," answered Radford, involuntarily getting upon the counter to be out of the way of the bull-dog. "A spotted hound pup. Have you seen anything of it?"

"Is it that yer asking?" demanded the Hibernian, with a scowl, and indicating the dog with his stick. "Isn't he here, safe as iver, and a beauty he is, more be token!"

"*That* dog? that isn't mine!" said Radford. "What in thunder do I want of *that?*"

"Sorra wan of me knows what yer wantin' of it!" replied the visitor. "All I know is that ye sthuck up a bit uv writing on the tree beyant, sayin' that ye'd been losing a dog, and one o' the min who could rade a bit, read it to me, and I've brought the dog and am wantin' me money!"

"I tell you that is not my dog!" said Radford, now not only vexed but discouraged.

"An' I till you that it *is* your dog!" bellowed the Hibernian. "Divil a bit can you come yer thricks over Jemmy Byrne! Didn't ye put it in the writin' that ye'd lost a dog, and here I have brought ye *wan* [one]! Didn't yez say that yer dog was spotted, and look at that, now! Jest mind what a fine timper he has!" At this moment the brute gave a growl that showed how willingly he would have made a meal of the clerk on the counter.

"Just take him out of here, will you?" said Radford. "I tell you he isn't mine, and I don't want anything to do with him."

"But be the Hill of Howth, I'm not going to take him out of here, and divil a step will I stir till I get me money!" persisted the visitor, who took occasion at that moment to stir up the animal with his stick and elicit another growl. "Yez don't be desaving poor men in that manner, takin' the likes of me away from me wurruk, to bring yer dirty dogs to yez, and thin refusin' to pay up like min—more shame to yez!"

"I won't pay a cent, and I want that dog taken out of here, at once!" said Radford, who nevertheless felt a little pale about the gills and wished that some big customer would happen in.

"Thin be the sowl of Molly Kelly I'll let the baste take the worth of the money out of yez!" yelled the Hibernian, and he made a motion to loosen the rope from his neck.

"Stop," said poor Billy, seeing no help approaching. "The dog isn't mine, and I don't want him, but I have no objection to paying you a little something for your trouble."

"Well, that's raysonable, anyway!" said the visitor, desisting from his intention of untying the dog. "How much wud ye give?"

"I can't afford much," answered Radford, "but say a dollar or two—"

"Five wudn't be too much for all me throuble," said the sturdy ditch-man, "and I couldn't think of looking at a dirty *wan*; but if ye'd make it three—"

"I'll just give you two, if you'll take that dog away, or you may go to the d—l, and I'll try cheese-knife against dog!" was the ultimatum of Radford.

"Well, yez may hand it over here," replied the dog-conducter, "only yez need niver expict *me* to bring yez another dog!"

"And I hope to the Lord you never *will!*" was the reply of Radford, as he sprung down from the counter on the back side, took out a two dollar bill from the drawer and threw it over. The Hibernian picked it up, examined it as if he knew a bank-bill from a shinplaster, growled over it a little, then thrust it into his pocket, gave the dog another punch that brought a growl and a half spring out of him, tautened the leading-string on the animal, and departed—Billy breathing very much freer when he disappeared up the road.

He had no more applications that day, nor did he hear anything of his missing pup. It is only fair to the young man to say that he did not make many more enquiries about it, the dog-fever having now calmed considerably.

But that night—the story of the night-bell and the mistake of the hurt man and the dog having no doubt got abroad,—there was a general irruption of disturbance in that direction. Half a dozen of the roughest practical jokers in the section, having got in leading-strings half a dozen of the ugliest curs in the country, visited the night-bell and rung him up. When he came down, he certainly had his choice among a collection of canine quadrupeds that would have frightened the witches in Macbeth into greater ugliness. From this visitation, which was a jocular one, Radford was relieved after bringing out a spread of crackers, cheese, raisins, cakes and wine, from the grocery department, which really did not cost *him* much, but mortified him excessively and increased his chances of some day having an unpleasant settlement with the proprietor.

The next day, after seeing that the notices were down, under the plea of ill-health he procured leave of absence for a week; and if any more dogs were brought for his acceptance he did not see them.

When he returned, at the end of that time, the incident had pretty much blown over, and—*he did not want any dog*. The kennel made splendid kindling-wood. I am not aware that the mystery of the disappearance of the pup was ever cleared away—whether some dog-fancier had stolen him, or whether the proprietor, tired of his noise and botheration, had procured or connived at his disappearance. I imagine that this part of the affair will ever rest in the same darkness that shrouds the names of the builders of the Pyramids, the Author of Junius, and the Man who kissed Sally Farrell.

VII.

CAPTAIN CRABBE AND HIS SPECULATION IN HARNESS.

"Quiz" was the only one word in the language capable of expressing the character of Captain Tom Crabbe in the day when I know him best. He spent three-quarters of his life, it appeared to me, in the effort to discover some means by which his neighbors could be harmlessly overreached and made pleasantly uncomfortable; and his well-to-do situation in the world and the abundance of leisure he enjoyed, placed him in precisely the position to make his search successful. He carried on some maritime business, but mostly through other hands, and so managed that his boats and boatmen made money for him, while he remained ashore, took his apparent ease, and merely acted as that most important of all things in any line of business—a *manager*.

When the Captain's showy velvet vest and enormous guard chain, which were the first things to be observed about him in those days, hove in sight,—those who knew him began to be careful about their conversation, and "mind their eyes" generally, well aware that if they did not they would fall victims to some wholesale joke at all the stores, shops and taverns in the village, before the hours were many. Let me do him the justice to say that his jokes were all sunshine and no lightning—that they tickled and sometimes scorched, but never scathed and blighted—and that the village droll well earned the right to all the pranks he played, by a hand as "open as the day to melting charity," and a heart that never closed against the appeal of suffering. Was a poor fellow missing from his home one afternoon, and his body found on the shore next morning, a helpless wife and children left behind him;—or did another fall across the great circular-saw of the timber yard and lose a hand or two or three fingers, disabling him and throwing his family into want,—did any of these things occur, Captain Tom was to be found going about town, merry and quizzical as usual, but with a relief list which he himself had nobly headed, and laughing the quarters and halves out of people's pockets with more facility than others could have wept and begged them out of the same entrenchment.

No one, resident at that time within forty miles of the marine village, will forget the tricks Captain Tom habitually played upon a pompous numscull of a lawyer residing near him and doing his miserable little to involve the community in litigation. Scarcely a week passed but Captain Tom would set him on the scent of a scandal, which, followed up, would result in a sad disappointment if not a tweaked nose,—or befog him with an array of bogus papers and documents over which he would pore and puzzle for days without discovering either the meaning of the papers or the "sell" which had been practised upon him. Once he sent the same enthusiastic individual the whole length of the State, to try his chances for United States Senator before the joint-meeting of the legislature, on the pretended wish of the Governor that he should do so; and at another time he manufactured a case of piracy in the robbery of an oyster sloop lying in the neighborhood, of a pair of old boots, a hat and some bed-clothes, especially to see with what vim and energy the legal ninny would strive for the conviction of the imaginary offender.

Then a spread-eagle sort of young fellow, who was very loud and troublesome, and who had attained the dignity of Marshal of a Fourth of July parade by being in everybody's way so that he was stuck on a horse to get clear of him,—was invited to accept a sword which his grateful townsmen had voted to his "dignity and efficiency on the occasion." The sword was kept concealed from the recipient and all his friends, and at the appointed time the village Academy was thronged to witness the presentation. The sword, which was presented by the Captain, in a speech the pregnant matter of which made up for its want of length,—the sword, on being unrolled from its voluminous wrappings on the great occasion in question, after the presentation speech had been made and the stupid recipient had run himself into the proper scrape by acknowledging it,—proved to be one beaten out of an old iron-hoop by Briggs, the blacksmith, who was an able aid-de-camp to Crabbe—the handle formed of an immense sugar-beet!

Fires—burglaries—immense transactions in land, and other like speculations—horse races between horses that could no more run than so many cows—boat races between boats that could no more sail than a Susquehanna lumber raft—mass-meetings with flaming hand-bills, for purposes of which no one ever before heard,—these made up a considerable part of the Captain's stock in trade, in the good old days. Occasionally, but very rarely, he took a slight property advantage when the chance offered, but never to an amount exceeding what even the victim would regard as a "good joke" and a "fair sell." Only once do I remember his meeting his match in that direction; and that instance will bear relating more particularly.

Captain Crabbe had, at the period referred to, a very nice sett of single harness, just finished off by Rube Ferret, the saddler, to the tune of fifty dollars, and had not yet taken them home. When he did take possession of them, in a few days, they were to be devoted to ornamenting and setting off the glossy sides of his little bay pony, and create some sensation as he dashed through the town in a spruce buggy just turned out by the village wheelwright. Passing by Haskell's baker-shop, one afternoon, when he knew that the harness must be finished, a bright idea struck Captain Tom, with which his eyes fell privately into their merriest twinkle. Of all the world, Rube himself, an incarnate mischief, was the person on whom a "sell" would tell the best in the village, and forthwith the machinery was put in operation. He saw Ferret and Haskell in conversation at the door, and strolled negligently over.

A day or two before, Captain Crabbe had been in the city on business, and tempted by the display in a jeweller's window on Greenwich street, he had invested forty dollars in a plain chatelaine chain probably worth the full amount he had paid for it. This, on the afternoon in question, was conspicuously displayed by being hooked in the bottom buttonhole of his showy vest, and had been making quite a sensation all day among those he met.

After a word or two of conversation with Ferret and Haskell, Captain Tom appeared suddenly to remember that he had an appointment, and pulled out his lever, taking care that the heavy chain should remain dangling in his hand long enough to attract the attention of Rube. The eye of the latter caught the chain, and the Captain saw the twinkle. He gave his watch a loud snap, and gathered up his chain as if about to put it back into his pocket.

"Nice chain!" remarked Rube, falling into the very train of thought the Captain could have wished.

"Ya-a-a-s," said the Captain, drawing the word out as if he meant to be understood that he had no particular thought on the subject, and that it was a matter of very little consequence.

"Got it lately?" asked Rube, who seemed really taken by the chain.

"Yes," answered the Captain, "got it only a day or two ago, in the city."

"Nice chain—very nice chain," again repeated Ferret. "Wouldn't mind if I had one just like it, myself. Gold, I suppose?"

"Humph!" said the Captain, "pure gold, of course, or I wouldn't wear it! I bought it for myself, but—well, you can have it if you want it."

"Oh, no," answered Ferret—"I should like to have it well enough, but I can't afford it."

"You *could* afford it in trade, couldn't you?" asked the Captain.

"Well, I don't know," said Ferret, slowly. "Trade? well, perhaps I could."

"Humph, well!" spoke the Captain, quickly, as if he had just thought about it. "I can get another when I go up again. Tell you what I'll do. I'll give you this chain, *now*, for the best sett of harness in your shop."

Ferret seemed to hesitate a moment, but the Captain hurried him up with:

"Come, speak quick if you want it! I'm going to the city again pretty soon, and I must go, now."

"Well, I'll take it!" answered Ferret. Whereupon Captain Tom, unhooking the chain from his watch, handed it over, suppressing the inward chuckle which shook him to the toes of his boots, and taking the precaution to put Haskell in the position of witness by saying:

"You understand, Haskell? I give Rube my chain, and he is to give me, for it, the best sett of single harness in his shop!"

"I understand," said Haskell, and "It's all right!" said Rube, putting the chain in his pocket.

Rube Ferret suddenly saw somebody beckoning him, at that moment. from the door of his own shop, and walked away, leaving Captain Tom still with Haskell.

"Do you know where I've got him?" asked Captain Tom, who, now that the trade was duly accomplished, was ready to begin "roasting" Ferret all over town.

"No," said Haskell.

"Well, I'll tell you, then!" laughed the Captain. "I paid forty dollars for that chain, a day or two ago, and it is about worth the money. Ferret has been making me a sett of fifty dollar single harness, and they are done, but I haven't taken 'em home! Don't you see? Ferret did not think about *my* harness, and *I have got my fifty dollar harness for forty dollars!*"

"Ha! ha! ha! capital!" laughed Haskell," Yes, you have got him nicely!" and the Captain strolled off to tell the story at the oyster-saloon on the corner. While he was telling it, some one called his attention.

"Why what a turn-out you are making, Captain Crabbe! Your son Joe has just gone by, with the pony to a new buggy, and all rigged up in a new harness that shines like a button!"

"New harness!—the devil he is!" roared the

Captain, running to the door, something striking him violently in the perceptive organs about that moment. "Joe has got the new harness!—oh, Lord, I'll be the death of him!" and away he went down the street after the offending Joe.

Ferret happened along again by Haskell's shop a few moments afterwards, his new chain dangling beautifully.

"Eh, Haskell," said Rube, "do you know the joke?"

"No!" answered Haskell—"except that the Captain seems to have got a fifty-dollar harness out of you for a forty-dollar chain!"

"Has he?" laughed Rube. "I know what he paid for the chain—Joe told me. Got me, has he? Do you remember the bargain? He was to have the best single harness in my shop for the chain. I suppose he *thought* HIS fifty-dollar harness was in my shop, but it wasn't: Joe came and took it away this morning! *The best single harness in my shop is just worth twenty-five dollars!*"

"Oh, ho! ho—oh, ho! oh!" laughed Haskell, doubled up over his own counter. Very much after the same order the whole crowd at the saloons and the taverns laughed half an hour afterwards when the transaction became fairly known. It cost the Captain a round sum in the way of "wetting" his bargain, the same afternoon and evening, and many a long day went by before he even temporarily heard the last of his speculation in harness.

VIII.

BURSTING UP A QUORUM.

THE Board of Aldermen of a certain prominent city on the Western Continent, notorious for its lavish expenditure of money at all times, and of men in time of war—had a vacant chair a few seasons ago, which remained unfilled for many months. I happened at the time to hold the highly responsible and lucrative position of fifth-wheel-of-the-coach to that honorable body; and even in that high place, where the dignity of the city was supposed to be resting in all confidence, I occasionally saw a bit of drollery worth recording. The most marked was in connection with the vacancy just mentioned.

Alderman J—— G——, of the ——th district, died suddenly not long after his election, leaving that vacant chair to be draped in funeral crape and stared wonderingly at by the people in the lobby. For certain reasons, there was no intention whatever on the part of the board, of ordering an election to fill the vacancy. The full board numbered seventeen, and as then constituted it stood nine democrats to seven republicans, with a democrat of course in the chair, and one of the democrats a little doubtful when it came to close voting. The ——th district was known to be republican, and if the vacancy should be filled the board would stand nine and eight, with one of the majority not to be depended upon in emergencies. This would be decidedly too close work, and accordingly the majority kept the place vacant. Resolution after resolution had been introduced by the minority, ordering an election in the ——th district, but each had been so conclusively voted down that the matter was considered hopeless and dropped by general consent.

One evening of the fall of 185–, however, there was a sudden change in the programme. One of the democratic members had gone to Europe during the summer and had not yet returned ; another was out-West on business ; and one or two more did not happen to make their appearance. Result—the board found itself in session on that evening, for a wonder, *with a republican majority*. All the seven republicans were present, with five democrats, making twelve members present in all—nine being the necessary quorum for the transaction of business. Not long after the usual routine business of the session had been transacted, I saw that there was mischief ahead of some character. The republican leaders were whispering together and chuckling a little, and one or two mysterious slips of paper passed from one end of the long circular desks to the other. Then I saw blank looks suddenly fall upon the faces of the democratic leaders, and I knew that they too saw the brewing mischief. President Lancey, (that name will do as well as any other for the occasion) a keen-faced, thin and wiry young man, and one of the ablest presiding officers I have ever seen in any body, was drawing his moustache down a little nervously, and I could see that he was biting his lips. Directly the blow fell, in a resolution sent up to the President's desk and handed me to read aloud:

"*Resolved*, That the Clerk of this Board be directed to issue the proper notifications for an election for a member of this Board from the ——th district of this city, to fill the vacancy occasioned by the death of Alderman J—— G——, said election to take place on the —— day of ——, 185—."

Phew! here was a thunderbolt, indeed! The minority had temporarily become the majority, from the default of the latter; and they had determined to ignore the usual courtesies shown by a minority when *accidentally* placed in the majority in this way, and force an election in the vacant district. They clearly had the power for the moment, and quite as clearly they were determined to exercise it to the full extent. Would they succeed? That remained to be seen.

I think that by this time one of the five democrats had gone home for the evening, unconscious of any danger, leaving only four to oppose the seven republicans. That four was composed of President Lancey, before mentioned, keen, though *clerkly* and even *editorial*, and as sharp a political manager and parliamentarian as one needs to meet on a summer's day; Poole, the most effective managing floor member I have ever seen in any deliberative body, excellent at building a political *craft*, and considered to "carry a good many guns," if not to exercise the influence of a *Controller*, in nominating conventions; Haddam, a moderate partizan and a clever fellow, who delighted in throwing occasional shots into Poole and others, which sometimes *moved the house;* and a fourth, whose personality I have really forgotten. I have partially forgotten, too, who were the republican leaders on the occasion, but judging from the date they must have been Rucker,

Sparr, Breed and Admiral Wynes, or some names very like them.

Lancey saw the full danger in a moment. So did Poole. Up sprang the latter the moment the resolution was done reading.

"I move that this board do now adjourn!"

"Aye!" "aye!" "aye!" cried the two or three other democrats; but "no!" "no!" "no!" came back from the other side of the house, and much more plentifully.

"Ayes and noes!" demanded Poole, who evidently meant to fight it out, and to gain all the time possible, in the hope that some other diversion might be effected. The ayes and noes were taken, and the vote stood four for adjournment and seven against. So the board did not adjourn.

"I move that the resolution just read be adopted," said one of the republicans. "Question!" "question!" cried one of the others, determined to shut off all debate if such a thing was possible.

"Not so fast!" said Poole. "Mr. President, I move a reconsideration of the vote just taken," (on the adjournment).

"Nonsense!" said one of the republicans.

"We will see whether it is nonsense!" answered Poole. "Mr. President, I move for a reconsideration."

President Lancey, whose eyes began to twinkle with mischief, begged the indulgence of the board for a few minutes, while he looked into some authorities lying on the desk, on the parliamentary question whether a motion to reconsider a lost vote for adjournment was strictly in order. He occupied about a quarter of an hour in making the research, while the republicans fidgeted and the democrats thought that they began to see daylight. He then decided that according to "Jefferson's Manual" and other books, which he had been consulting, he thought that a motion to reconsider a lost vote on an adjournment could *not* be entertained. It is scarcely necessary to say that he had not been looking between the covers of any work on parliamentary usage, and that he knew what "Jefferson's Manual" would say on so ridiculous a subject, quite as well before looking as after.

"Question!" "question!" again cried some of the republicans.

"The question will be on the resolution offered by the Alderman from the —th," said the President, rising very gravely. "Are you ready for the question?"

"I move that the resolution be referred to the Committee on Arts and Sciences," said Haddam.

"There is a motion already before the board, and of course such a motion cannot be in order," said one of the republicans.

"Eh, isn't it, Mr. President?" added Haddam, as gravely as if he did not know better.

"No," said the President, "the gentleman from the ——th is out of order. The question will be on the——"

"I believe a motion to *amend* is in order; isn't it, Mr. President?" said Poole, looking as defiantly at the President as if he thought that official had just been doing him a gross personal injury.

"It is," said the President.

"Then I move," said Poole, "to amend the resolution by substituting for the date therein named, the 29th day of December, 185—," naming a time just two days before the expiration of the term for which the new member would be elected.

Amid the cries of "shame," "humbug," &c., from the republicans, President Lancey gravely put the question on the amendment, which was pretty plainly lost. Then Haddam called for the ayes and noes, which were taken, and the amendment declared lost by four to seven.

At this stage, other business having intervened so as to make such a motion again in order, Poole moved "that this board do now adjourn," on which the ayes and noes were again taken, with the same result as before. More cries of "question!" "question!" from the republicans, who evidently had not faltered a whit in their intention to force the matter through, albeit it was now growing a little late. Poole, finding his other tactics driven to the wall, now rose to speak on the main question. As may be supposed, his principal intention was to "speak against time," in the hope of worrying out the opposition, and he did not stint himself in the way of introduction, explanation or apology. In about half an hour of earnest declamation he cleared away the surrounding obstructions, and succeeded in getting into the neighborhood of his subject. By that time the lobby was partially cleared, and two of the reporters had gone to sleep at the table. Then he launched into a historical examination of the rules governing public bodies—cited instances from the history of the Senate of Rome, to prove that no public body was considered to be any the less completely constituted on account of the absence of one or more of its members, provided there was a quorum for the transaction of the public business, etc.

At this stage one of the republicans (probably Alderman Rucker) fell into the trap of helping Poole along. He interrupted that orator to show him that keeping the people of the ——th district without a representative in the board, while they were taxed for the support of the city government, was precisely that system of "taxation without representation," which brought on the troubles between the colonies and the mother country, and that such a course struck at the very foundation of the rights of freemen.

Then Poole used a quarter of an hour to apologise to the board for his inadvertence in that particular, and to admit the gentleman's very correct view of the subject, *under some circumstances*, but not in circumstances like the present, when the city was to be saddled with the heavy expense of a special election without due cause.

By this time the reporters had woke up and gone away; President Lancey had picked his teeth and pared his nails until there was no longer any excuse for continuing those operations; and Poole, fairly run out, managed to throw in a few personalities at one of the opposition. Up popped the attacked member, and called him to order. He insisted that he was in order, and the President decided that he was not, when Poole appealed from the decision of the chair and called the ayes and noes on the appeal. The chair was sustained, by a vote of seven to three, and Poole sat down, thoroughly beaten out, but after having managed to consume an hour and a quarter and made the time somewhere between ten and eleven o'clock.

At about this time the fourth of the democratic members, who had taken no share in the debates, though he had voted with the party—took his hat and left the chamber. One of the republican members, the moment after noticing he was gone, called attention to the fact, and intimated that he had "dodged" with the intention of defeating the obnoxious measure by leaving the board without a quorum.

"No, I guess not," said Poole, "I think he has only stepped down stairs for a moment. I'll have him back at all events, for I mean that this matter shall be met squarely." His face was so gravely conscientious, meanwhile, that the least credulous of men might have been excused for trusting him. He went out *without his hat*, to look for the absent member; but it seemed that he must have got lost in the intricate passages of the hall, for after the board had suspended business and waited for him at least a quarter of an hour, *he did not seem to come back*, much less bring the member of whom he had started in search.

At this stage of affairs one of the republican members became indignant, and rose to make a very short but very pithy speech.

"Mr. President," he said, "this conduct is outrageous! It is evidently the intention of certain members of this board to perpetuate an injustice, and prevent the public business being done, by leaving the board without a quorum. Two have already left the room within a few minutes, leaving us, as you will perceive, barely a quorum." (There were now present, it will be remembered, the President, Haddam and the seven republicans, making the necessary nine and not one to spare. If one more could manage to get away, the game would be up, effectually). "I call upon you, Mr. President," he went on—"I call upon you, as the executive officer of this board, to do your duty and prevent any other member leaving the room until adjournment."

"Certainly!" said President Lancey, rising with dignity and bending a sharp eye on the Sergeant-at-Arms, as if *he* had been at fault in permitting so many of the members to leave. "This conduct is entirely improper, and must not be repeated. Mr. Sergeant-at-Arms, keep that gate closed until you have orders to open it, and see that no other member leaves the chamber!"

The Sergeant-at-Arms nodded, and looked at the

fastenings of his iron gate. The republican faces relaxed: they yet had their rats in the trap, and there was really no escape.

"Question!" "question!" said one or two, again, confident that it could not be staved off any longer.

"One moment, if you please, gentlemen!" said President Lancey, "I may have a word or two to say upon this subject. Mr. Haddam, be kind enough to take the chair for a few minutes."

He came down from the President's chair, and Alderman Haddam went up and took the seat and the gavel. President Lancey took the same privilege which some of the others had during the evening, to speak from the centre of the open space between the desks; and as he had a loud voice and an effective utterance, he went pretty well down the circle towards the gate. Here he turned, looked towards the President *pro tem.*, fixed his sharp eye full on him, threw himself into an oratorical position, and commenced what was evidently intended to be *the* oration of his official term:

"Mr. President, on this important subject—"

Future ages will be under the necessity of waiting for the balance of this oration, as those present have done ever since; for making a sudden turn, two steps and a spring, the President who, among his accomplishments, numbered that of being a very respectable gymnast, went flying over the gate and over the head of the Sergeant-at-Arms, who sat faithfully beside it, and before human arm could arrest and almost before human eye could see he was out of the outer door and gone beyond pursuit.

"I don't think we have a quorum, call the roll, Mr. Clerk!" said Alderman Haddam, President *pro tem.* The roll was called, and only eight members answered. "A quorum not being present," the President said, coolly, and bringing down his mallet with a portentous rap that sounded the death-knell of the republican hopes for that occasion—"a quorum not being present, this board stands adjourned to Monday evening." About five minutes afterwards, seven remarkably sheepish looking Aldermen, and one who seemed very well content with himself and the world, might have been seen leaving the Aldermanic chamber, bearing the hats of Poole and the President, which they had captured and confiscated. And this was apparently all the aspect of the affair, but really far from it!

For it was only a day or two after that I met Poole, and commenced laughing with him over the occurrence. "A pretty close shave!" I said, "I thought at one time you were gone, and that they would have forced the vote and carried the resolution in spite of you!"

"Humph! did you?" said Poole, with a glance expressive of pity for any one who could be so verdant. "Did you, indeed? I don't think there was any danger, after *I* got away."

"Eh, why not?" I asked. "Suppose they had happened to detect Lancey in his gymnastic trick, and detained him? What would you have done *then?*"

"In that case," answered Poole, "as I was at that moment in the cellar, in intimate relation with the gas-metre, and with telegraphic communication above—if I found that Lancey could not make his escape, I should immediately have turned off the gas from the chamber, and I think he might have managed to get away while they were hunting up candles!"

I quite agreed with him; and at all events I was wiser then than before, as to the resources of professional politicians and the plans that can be put into operation by moral and physical gymnasts for bursting up a legislative quorum that may happen to have the wrong political complexion.

IX.

PILOTING WITHOUT A LICENSE.

Sanderson and I were "lying off," as the fast boys express it, on Smith's Island, that delightful retreat in the middle of the Delaware, opposite Philadelphia, where bathing is very free and where they sell excellent clam-soup as well as quite respectable ice-cream. The day was hot and Philadelphia was unendurable; and Sanderson had been guilty of a practical joke in the Empire City a few days previous, which made a temporary sojourn elsewhere desirable. As we lay kicking up our heels on the benches, one of the Camden ferry-boats, coming up to her slip, ran into a lighter, and the incident put me in mind to tell Sanderson Oakey Hall's capital story, told by the "Manhattaner in New Orleans," of Dick Benbow's experiment at amateur piloting, when he ran the Red River packet into the big Indiaman and caused such a commotion in and about the Crescent City.

"A very good story," said Sanderson, when I had finished, "and probably the longest as well as the biggest lie ever told on Smith's Island. However, it is none the worse for that, and some fellow who had a propensity for practical jokes might take a hint from it. In fact—well, no matter *what* is the fact. I once did a little amateur piloting myself, though only in a very small way, and on a sailing vessel."

"Ah!" I said, with interest. "Where, and how?"

"Coming up the Lower Bay of New York from the Fishing Banks, on a sloop," he replied. "Half a dozen of us had hired the sloop for a trip down, and coming in we got becalmed near the point of the Hook. Here we drifted about until after dark, and only crept up towards the Narrows at a snail's pace. We had a card table in the cabin, and played most of the evening, while the sloop was lazily rolling about between Romer Shoal and the West Bank. I got tired of the amusement after awhile, and went out. There was only a boy at the tiller; and a sleepy look out, if any, forward, as the captain and the two hands had gone down into the forecastle to supper.

"I have sometimes had a fancy that I could steer a boat, and that evening the fancy was particularly strong. I found the boy a little sleepy, the sloop within a couple of miles of the light at the Narrows, the wind very light from the south-east, and things generally quiet. I very soon suggested to him that *I* knew how to steer, and as he knew that I was one of the persons who had hired the boat, he made no objection to my taking the helm, merely remarking that I must keep her head as it was, with the Narrows light a little on the larboard bow. I promised care, and the little fellow was asleep in five minutes, under the quarter-rail.

"I don't know how it was—how I could possibly have lost that light, but lose it I did. Perhaps I was looking more at the stars than the course of the sloop, at one time. At all events, I kept a light which I supposed to be that of the light-house, on the larboaru bow, faithfully. I have reason to believe that the light-house got behind the sail somehow, and that I was steering for a light in one of the windows of some house back on the Staten Island bluff. The breeze from the south-east certainly freshened finely, and the little sloop was going through the water very nicely, when—"

"Well when what?" I asked impatiently.

"When my amateur pilotage came to a sudden conclusion. The sloop went ashore, head on, with a fresh breeze, on the Staten Island beach, about half way between the Narrows and the old Elm Tree, where there was at that time no light."

"Whew!" I said.

"Yes, 'whew' it was!" responded Sanderson. "I have an idea that the captain and men came out from supper, the men at the card table broke up and came out of the cabin, the look-out, if there was any, woke up forward, and my sailor-boy aft—very much at the same time. I cannot say exactly what occurred. We had been towing the yawl behind, and I knew that the oars were in her. I suppose it must have been a dastardly trick, to desert my comrades and carry off the only boat, at a time of shipwreck; but I did not think them in any great danger, on the Staten Island shore in a calm night; and certain it is that I let myself down by the davit-fall, about as quick as I would have absconded from the window of a house where I had been caught stealing; dropped in the water—clambered into the boat—cut her adrift—and rowed away to the shore, half a mile above, almost before any of them discovered the cause of the catastrophe."

"Recreant!" I said, in the pauses of my hearty guffaw over Sanderson's exploit.

"Recreant, of course!" he replied. "Any one always *is*, who manages to get out of a scrape and leave the others *in!* I slept at a Staten Island fish-hut, the balance of the night, after drying myself. The sloop had gone up pretty high, and one of the sailors waded ashore, found the boat, and ferried off the others. We all reached New York at about the same time the next morning. The sloop got off on a spring tide, within a week, and there was a small bill to pay for detention and repairs, which they all insisted that I should pay alone, and which I *didn't.* Pretty gratitude! to mulct me in damages for an accident occurring when I was daring the dangers of the sea as a volunteer, and the rest taking their pleasure!"

Of course I assented to his view of the case. Who would not, with so jolly a fellow as Sanderson? At about that time the sea-steamer John Smith made her landing at the Island, and we took passage on that noble craft for the foot of Walnut street. Sanderson seemed pre-occupied, and there was something in his face to indicate that his great soul was struggling with still greater thoughts. I did not for the time disturb him, confident that the pre-occupation would before long develope itself.

We dined at Bloodgood's, a hotel I have always had a weakness for selecting, as it furnishes capital plum pies for dinner all the year round, and lies so near the river that lazy people do not have any distance to travel when going on boat excursions. When we had finished dinner, and were enjoying the post-prandial cigar, Sanderson asked:

"Have you ever been down to Fort Mifflin?"

"Never," I replied. "Why? have you suddenly picked up an interest in fortification?"

"No," he rejoined, "but I saw a steamboat named the Ceres one or two piers below, that runs down there. Suppose we go down and look at the scenery."

"Well," I said; and we started. On the next block was a ship-chandler's store, and when opposite the door Sanderson stopped me.

"I have got an errand here," he remarked.

"Ropes? eh, what? not going to hang yourself?" I suggested.

"Not if I know it," was Sanderson's reply. "But still I have a purchase to make. Come in a moment."

We entered the store, and Sanderson inquired for "black hemp twine, very small." What the deuce could he want of it? He *said* that he wanted to make a fishing-line of it, but I had no idea that he was really going fishing. A ball of very fine, strong dark twine was produced. Sanderson paid a "bit" for it, then cut off probably twenty feet, and made the shop-keeper a present of the balance. He then asked for, procured and pocketed, half a pound of sheet-lead, for a "sinker," as he said. I now knew there was deviltry ahead, but had no idea what it could be, and my companion did not explain.

We went down the pier and on board the Ceres, then just off for Fort Mifflin, ten or a dozen miles down the Delaware. Arrived at the promenade-deck, on which there happened to be no one but ourselves for the moment, Sanderson unfolded the string and his intentions.

"Do you see that hook?" he asked, calling my attention to a bell-pull that lay perpendicularly along the flag-staff at the extreme stern, the hooked part downwards.

I remarked that I did, and volunteered the information that it was connected, by a wire running up the staff and along one of the rails of the promenade-deck covering, with the engine-room, and that it was put there for the purpose of enabling the captain or pilot, in case either happened to be astern, and any one fell overboard or any other accident happened which might require the boat to be suddenly stopped,—to ring the engineer's bell without delay.

"Just so," said Sanderson. "Now I'm not the captain, but the pilot, as we were talking a while ago. You have just put me in the notion of it, by your New Orleans story, and I am going to ring that bell when I get ready."

"When?"

"When we get out in the stream," he replied.

"And with the—"

"With the string, of course," he replied. "You don't suppose that I am fool enough to stand up here and be caught in the operation?"

"But the consequences—you do not know what damage you may do?" I began to say.

"Do you know what Dick Benbow remarked, in the story you were telling?" he replied. "Now I say emphatically with him, 'the devil take the consequences.' I won't ask you to help; all I want is that you should keep still, if you don't want to be murdered!"

Under such circumstances, of course, I promised to "keep still," and the drama proceeded.

The Ceres had left the dock by this time, and was out in the stream. A considerable number of persons were coming up on the promenade, and distributing themselves along the seats. Sanderson took his seat beside the flag-staff, with myself at the left, and smoked rapidly. Then adroitly doubling the twine, he hooked the bight or double of it over the bell-pull, and let the two ends drop down towards the railing below. The cord was very fine and small, and no casual observer would have been at all likely to see it. Sanderson got up from his seat, remarking that we had both lost our lights, and that we must go below and replenish. I followed him, I confess with some feeling of trepidation, for I never know precisely when a practical joke comes to an end, much more than I do how much damage a wild bull may do, let out in a crowd.

Arrived below, Sanderson nudged me again, and we went back to the extreme stern of the main deck, in the narrow space occupied by the anchor, between the railing and the saloon bulkhead. Fortunately (or unfortunately) there was no one in the way, and the two ends of the cord hung quietly down within reach. The steamboat was now well off from the town, but pretty well surrounded by steamboats and ferry-boats, and with a few sloops and schooners beating down against the breeze from the southward.

"I think now is about the time!" said Sanderson, and before I could expostulate, and almost before I could think, he gave a violent jerk at the two ends of the cord which he had caught in his hand. "Cling!" went the gong in the engine room, and we could distinctly hear the sound astern. The motion of the boat slowed instantly. Another jerk, the moment after. "Cling!" went the gong again, and the engine stopped very hurriedly. Then there was a sound of the gong which must have come from the pilot-house and was probably the single pull of the bewildered pilot to go-ahead. But I am not clear as to what occurred. Sanderson was getting in a hurry, and he gave the cords two sudden jerks. "Cling—cling!" went the gong, and the puzzled engineer must have made an attempt to back her a little too suddenly, for something gave way with a crash in the engine-room, and in an instant the Ceres began to blow steam. With a celerity worthy of a better cause, Sanderson instantly let go one end of the cord, jerked hard on the other—it came down into his hands—and before I could tell what he intended, he had wrapped the string around the sheet-lead and dropped it quietly overboard.

At this moment there was a general scream from the upper deck, and at about the same time Sanderson and myself left the stern with some rapidity. It appears that we must have been crossing the bow of a large topsail schooner running on-a-wind, that had been hidden by the wood-work of the saloon from Sanderson and myself. Of course the sudden stoppage of the steamboat brought her full in the course of the schooner; and at this period her flying-jib-boom and bowsprit struck the Ceres on the starboard quarter of the saloon, sending everybody forward in a hurry, and carrying away everything clean to the deck on that part of the boat. The schooner had fortunately been filled away the instant those on board of her perceived that the steamboat had stopped, and she did not strike our hull. Had she done so, at the speed she was going, or had we been six feet farther astern, we should have been instantly sunk, without a question.

To say that I was frightened, in the midst of the crash and the uncertainty how much damage had been done to the boat and in the engine-room—and among the curses, screams and general confusion that resulted,—would be a very moderate admission. I caught a glimpse of Sanderson's face at the moment of the crash; it may have expressed fright, but if it did the feeling was so covered up beneath an expression of calm content and arduous duty well-accomplished, that I could not see it.

I cannot very well relate what happened afterwards. Of course no one but ourselves knew how the accident occurred, or who could have rung the bell. It is to be presumed that neither of us was communicative on the subject. The disabled and mutilated Ceres was soon surrounded by steamboats, ferry-boats and row-boats, and the passengers taken off, Sanderson and myself included. For some cause, undefinable even by ourselves, we went to Baltimore by the evening train. I doubt whether, to this day, (and several years have since elapsed) —any outsider has ever been aware of the origin of the accident, or guessed how much the owners of the good steamboat Ceres owed to Sanderson's last experiment at *piloting without a license.*

X.

THE MAJOR'S HORSE-OPERATION.

I HAPPENED to make the acquaintance of both the principal actors in the short story I am about to tell, a few months ago, on a lazy afternoon spent with a droll friend at South Brooklyn, and to be a spectator of a considerable part of the operation, the balance of which was supplied by the best authority.

Both the principal dramatis personæ are well known in certain sections, but as they may not have the world-wide celebrity which they really deserve, I must tell who and what they are.

"Pancake Johnny" is a contractor for removing certain embankments and other inconveniences lying in the way of opening certain streets, by the means of which Brooklyn is swallowing half Long Island and extending itself to the sea. "Pancake" employs a good many horses and carts, and has quite an extensive stable attached to his tumble-down premises on the—well no matter what avenue.

He has acquired his queer soubriquet by turning out all the women from his kitchen, years ago, and attending to the cooking of breakfast for his army of hands—himself; and by persisting in the habit of giving everybody, young and old, winter and summer, year after year—pancakes for breakfast. "Pancake" does not do any of the carting himself — only oversees it; and among his weaknesses is one for very quiet horses, and horses in good condition—I mean such horses as he wishes to drive himself, in his explorations among his contracts and his occasional visits to Brooklyn or Jamaica.

"The Major" is a different stripe of man, altogether. He is a darkey of the blackest type, small in stature, and with a cunning and yet good-humored leer about the mouth and eyes. He is an unmitigated horse jockey, and so recognized by all who know him, though he enjoys a fair reputation as that sort of a horse-dealer who, when you trust him and put him "on his honor," will not cheat you over three hundred per cent.

"The Major" has only a small amount of capital on hand, and buys his stock in small quantities; but he generally manages to turn it so rapidly that his pocket is not long empty, and that his little stable on forty something ——th street, Gowanus, seldom has the same horses within it one day and the next.

Pancake had been troubling the Major for some time to bring him a "nice pair of carriage horses." The Major had tried, and tried again in vain, by various purchases at Bull's Head and in other quarters, to meet the demand. One pair that he would take to Pancake would be too lively, another not fat enough, a third seemed too old, &c., &c., until the Major was almost in despair.

Finally, the Major came across a team of broken-down hacks, fatted up like hogs, and sent to the Bull's Head to be disposed of. His practised eye marked them at once, and he thought that they would exactly suit his friend. One hundred dollars and a little close chaffering bought the pair. Two hours afterwards they were at the Major's stable, and an hour later he drove them up to Pancake's.

"Jes look a here!" said the Major. "Massa Johnny, tink I got 'em things to suit you dis ere time!"

"Eh!" said Pancake, who was really taken with the looks of the hog-fat quiet old cobs. "Eh, yes, well, they *do* look pretty well; what do you ask for them?"

"Three hundred dollars!" said the Major, giving his whip a flourish which did not startle either one of them from its propriety—"been lookin' for 'em awful long while—purpose for you. Got 'em dis morning, and brought 'em right ober."

"Three hundred!" said Pancake, "couldn't think of it! I like 'em pretty well, but couldn't give over two hundred!"

"Now look a' here, Massa John," said the Major, imploringly, "don't be hard on a poor nigga! Paid two hundred and fifty for 'em dis mornin', 'specially for you. Ef I don't get any more dan dat, I don't make nuffin!"

The bait took with Pancake, but as he made it a rule never to pay the asking-price when it could be avoided, a little chaffering was necessary.

"Give you two hundred and fifty, and not a cent more!" was his ultimatum.

"Well, take 'em!" said the Major, after the necessary pause and hesitation. "'Spose I can make anudder trade in a day or two, 'fore dis nigga starves!" So the money was paid, and the Major left.

Pancake put his new horses in the stable, and was happy. Two days afterwards, when he went into the stable to harness them up for a ride, his satisfaction was considerably diminished. One of them had stood idle a little *too* long, and something of his natural character came out. He had got loose in the stables, nearly eaten up a colt in a neighboring stall, and kicked things to pieces generally.

Pancake made a muster of all the forces at his disposal, and managed to get his truculent steed penned up in a vacant stall apart from the others, where they threw in the feed to him and poured in his water through a trough. The same afternoon Pancake sent word to the Major to "come and take that horse away, right off, before he killed somebody."

The Major protested his astonishment, as he "had only had the hosses for an hour or two, and couldn't have knowed nuffin about 'em!" He promised, however, that if he could find another that he thought would suit Pancake, he would try to make a trade for him, and with this the latter was obliged to be content.

Two weeks later, when walking through the stalls at Bull's Head, the Major found another "magnificent steed"—a fine looking horse of middle age, with the "heaves" to so great an extent that he could hardly walk up to the watering-trough.

If there was anything that the Major *could* do, it was to "doctor" a horse for "heaves," and in a few minutes the horse was bought for thirty-seven dollars and fifty cents, and duly transferred, after dark, to the Major's stable. Here he was "treated" by the Major to a course of ginger, "heave-powders," &c., and in three days had a stock of wind on hand sufficient to last him, with moderate exercise, for a whole day.

Then the Major finished arrangements. He employed a half-Dutch young fellow, not known much in the neighborhood, and who was generally loafing at a tavern a few miles toward Jamacia,—to act as confederate in the delicate matter of trading horses with Pancake, aware that the latter might have some natural suspicions of any animal *he* brought.

Dutch was to receive five dollars for his share in the operation, and his role was as follows: He was to drive slowly down the road past Pancake's, and at a certain time, drive up when called by the Major, understand no English, and talk none except "seventy-five dollars to boot." The Major rigged him up in an old sulky, for the part, and then strolled leisurely along toward Pancake's.

"Well, you nigger," said Pancake, as soon as he saw the Major, "I thought you was going to get me another horse in the place of that one that eats up everybody! He ain't no use to me—haven't used him a stroke since I had him."

"Look a' here, Massa John," answered the Major, "de fac am, I has been looken for a nice hoss for you, ever sence, but didn't find him. Dis mornin' I *did* see a nice hoss, but—"

"But what?" asked Pancake, "couldn't you get him?"

"Oh, didn't try, Massa John," said the Major. "One of dem Dutch farmers had him, to a sulky, tied afore de tavern above. He was specious nice hoss, Massa John: ef you only could ha' seen him, now!"

"I should like to see him," said Pancake, who would have liked to see *anything* that promised him riddance of his plague.

"Mebbe he's comin' dis way," said the Major, "he was on the avenue, wid his head dis way. Well, I clar to gracious!" the Major continued, catching a glimpse of Dutch, who at that moment hove in sight, going at a jog trot with the horse. "Well, if that ain't lucky. Dere's de berry feller, now!"

"Are you sure?" asked Pancake.

"Sure? well I guess I am!" said the Major. "Dere ain't many such looking hosses as *dat*, around."

In a few moments Dutch came opposite, and the Major at once commenced swinging his hat and hallooing:

"Heah! look a heah, you! Just drive up heah!"

Dutchy heard and saw him, after a proper delay, and drove up. Pancake and the Major took a full survey of the horse, Dutch looking on with his mouth open and terribly astonished. Pancake and the Major exchanged private signs of approval.

"Nice horse," said the Major to Dutch.

"Yaw!" said Dutch, making a movement to go on.

"Want to trade, eh?" asked the Major.

"Nein Anglaishe sprachen!" said Dutch.

"Go bring out your horse," the Major suggested to Pancake, who obeyed.

"Want to trade? swap 'em?" asked Pancake of Dutch.

"Nein! nein!" answered Dutch vigorously. "Nix goot swop!"

"How much will you take to swop 'em?" asked the Major.

"Now Major, you had better go away," said Pancake, "he may know you as a horse-jockey, and be afraid to trade. Go off, and let *me* deal with him."

"Tink him afraid of dis nigger, eh?" said the Major. "Well, I'll go if you say so, only don't give him too much boot!" and the Major sauntered away to a drinking-house a block below, from which he had a fair view of the scene of bargaining without being seen himself.

He saw any quantity of motions, Pancake speaking rapidly, and Dutch shaking his head nearly all the time. At length Dutch nodded two or three times, and Pancake quietly rubbed his hands: the Major knew that the bargain was concluded, and ordered a brandy sling to celebrate the event. Then he saw Pancake go into his rookery, come out and put something into Dutch's hand. Then they unharnessed Dutch's horse, put Pancake's in its place, the latter led his new acquisition into the stable, and Dutch drove on down the road towards Fort Hamilton. The Major celebrated again.

An hour after the horse just got from Pancake was in the Bull's Head stables—the Major not judging it politic to let it be seen in *his*; Dutch was paid his five dollars and went away for a "high old drunk."

After the Major went away, it appeared Dutch had demanded "one huntred tollar" as boot, upon which Pancake offered fifty, and they finally "split the difference" at seventy-five.

Two days afterwards the Major met Pancake, with his new purchase and another horse before a light wagon, laboring up a slight hill towards New Utretcht, the new horse unable to go faster than a walk, and heaving at a rate which would have supplied blacksmiths' bellows for a county.

"Why, what on airth's de matter?" asked the Major, surprised.

"Matter!" said Pancake, with two or three bad words interspersed, "why, that cussed Dutchman has traded me a horse that isn't worth a cop! Hear how he blows, and he can't go off a walk, no how he can fix it!"

"Well, dat *is* too bad, Massa John!" said the Major, "but look a' heah, you wouldn't trust dis nigger, and wanted to trade for youseff! Just let dis nigger ha' stayed, and you wouldn't ha' been cheated!"

"No, I suppose not," said Pancake, starting on

his bellows, up hill ; but it is not clear that he meant that endorsement of the Major's integrity. He sold the new horse, two days after, for twenty-five dollars, to a clam-merchant, and the Major realized a hundred for his, at the Bull's Head, to a green Jerseyman. The Major has not furnished Pancake any stock since, or had not when I last heard from that locality.

XI.

THE LONG BRANCH MURDER.

"IT is devilish dull down here, devilish dull!" said one of the inmates of Blossom Lodge, that charming little club-house in the rear of Sammy Laird's Mansion House, Long Branch,—one morning a couple of summers ago, as he came out of the billiard-room under the Lodge, where he had been fighting after impossible caroms and investing very possible quarters. No matter what was the real name of the speaker—suffice it to say that he was one of the habitues of the Lodge—one of the set who for some years have been in the habit of running down about the first of July, and lounging about that paradise until the middle of September. When in the city he could be heard of not a thousand miles from the City Hall, and I shall call him for the occasion by a name immortalized by John Brougham—Smith.

The companion to whom he addressed that impatient remark, was another inmate of the Lodge, known as Captain Joe Darling, of the One Hundred and Sixth Ward Police. As everybody knows Captain Joe, I have not the least occasion for describing him or attempting to give his leading characteristics, except to say that the most desperate ruffians have a habit of shrinking away before his eye—that his bald head, when he uncovers it, gives him a venerable appearance which is not belied by the extreme gravity of his general demeanor—that his body, if one could but get a comprehensive view of it without the incumbrance of too much clothing, would show more scars won in the cause of justice, than many soldiers can show after passing through half a dozen bloody campaigns—that he is choice in the size and setting of his diamonds—and that he has a devoted love for fun, music, pantomime, and the New Bowery theatre.

"Dull, eh?" said Captain Joe, in reply to his companion's remark.

"Yes, devilish dull—and stupid!" said Smith. "I have got tired of going off fishing with those boatmen who charge two dollars for letting you burn yourself to a blister and wear all the skin off your hands. I have got tired of walking up and down the bank and the beach; and tired of riding over to Pleasure Bay to be upset in a small boat. All the women are dowdy or dignified, and I have a corn on my little toe which makes a hop detestable. Now you have just beaten me at billiards, and I was tired of them before. Heigho!"

"Humph!" said Captain Joe, "you must have been up a little late last night, with that party that went over to Shrewsbury, while Lance and I were reading all the evening like Christians and went to bed at ten."

"Oh no," said Smith, peevishly, "the fact is the *place* is dull! There is not a sensation within ten miles of it, and I am going up to the city to-morrow."

"Stop!" said Captain Joe, his face lighting up with some kind of a thought that was not far from inspiration. "Stop! don't go—at least don't go just yet. You want your tea a little stronger to-night, that is all, and you should have had a dash of Congress water this morning. Dull, eh?"

"Yes, dull!" repeated Smith, with a yawn.

"Well now, see here," said Captain Joe. "You and I haven't booked a bet since last election. Stay where you are for twenty-four hours, and then go to the city if you wish. Meanwhile I'll just bet you one even fifty that there is excitement enough on Long Branch, within that time, to satisfy even *you.*"

"Done," said Smith. "You are pretty fast, Joe, but you cannot scare up an excitement in that time, that will make a fellow's pulse beat faster by five to the minute."

"I'll try," said Captain Joe, "and if I don't succeed in satisfying you, just ask me for fifty after breakfast; and if I do, just pay over the same amount. Meanwhile, honor bright and hold your tongue, whatever you may see or hear—that is part of the conditions of the bet."

"Agreed," said Smith, and the two separated, Smith to look after some means of killing time for twenty-four hours more, and Captain Joe to corresponding arrangements for making it livelier.

Half an hour afterwards Captain Joe was walking up the bank, in close conversation with Lance, the patron of Blossom Lodge, a slight man with a bright face, a thin moustache, and an immense amount of blue flannel suit—and his lieutenant and comrade, commonly known as the "Colonel," a stouter built man with a round, good-humored face and a moustache that might have satisfied a member of Napoleon's Old Guard. Both Lance and the Colonel had more or less to do with official business in the city at the time—one in a highly lucrative and honorable position at the City Hall, and the other in a subordinate one in the brown stone building, which he has since exchanged for the service of the corporation inside the white marble.

What occurred between the three, can only be fancied, but that mischief was in the wind was most certain, from the drawing of Lance's mouth, the broad grins of the Colonel, and the quiet chuckles which shook Captain Joe to the ends of his boots. It is to be supposed that like a good general Captain Joe was issuing his orders for some great roguery that was to follow.

An hour afterwards the fishing-boats landed at the Fish-house above, and the Colonel strolled down to see the operation of weighing the fish, packing them in ice in the wagons, and sending them away for the inland and Philadelphia markets. Half an hour later, when the fish had all been disposed of, the Colonel, who had become pretty well acquainted with the fishermen, went up to Ab. Reed's with Sim Casey, a young snarer of sea-bass and porgies, and an unmarried man, who fished alone. They took a drink at the bar, which Casey thought a pleasant condescension on the part of the Colonel. Directly the Colonel inquired—

"How much do you average a day, Casey, at fishing?"

"Oh, from three to five dollars," said the fisherman.

"Do you want to do a job for me for twice the money, that will only take you the one day?"

"Suppose so," said Casey, "providing—"

"Oh, providing everything!" said the Colonel. "What I want you to do is just this. Go away to-night, to Deal, Squan, or anywhere, letting nobody see you go, and leaving your boat where she lies. Remain away until to-morrow afternoon—ask no questions, and here is your ten dollars. Of course there is a joke, but not on *you*, and I'll tell you all about it afterwards. Will you do it?"

"I'll do it!" said Casey.

"Make a big chalk-mark on the top of the stem of your boat, in the shape of a cross, so that it can be seen by moonlight," continued the Colonel—"and that is all."

Casey promised, and the Colonel wended his way back towards the Mansion House and his preparations for dinner.

That afternoon Lance ordered out his horses, and Captain Joe and himself drove up to Long Branch Village. Of course they had some errand there. Among other places that Captain Joe visited, was the butcher's. Then he went to the barber's and had a splendid shave. What else he did at either of the places, is among the mysteries yet to be revealed. If he brought away anything from either, he carried it in his pockets. Late in the afternoon the two drove back to the beach, and the evening passed away very much as usual. The night was a moonlight one, and Captain Joe may have strolled up the beach to enjoy it, as he often did—but if he did, nobody noticed him.

Morning, and a horrible sensation in the usually peaceful if not quiet precincts of the Long Branch boarding-houses. Startled messengers rushed in, bearing the intelligence that Sim Casey's boat had not gone off to the fishing-grounds that morning; that Sim Casey had disappeared and could not be found by any amount of enquiry; and that a dreadful murder had been committed, as a bloody club had been found in his boat, and mixed blood and hair on one of its sides. There could be no question, from the disappearance of the murdered man's body, that he had been induced to take some one or more off in the boat, by moonlight or very early in the morning—that he had been murdered there with the club, and thrown overboard—and that the murderers, in bringing the boat ashore, had forgotten to throw overboard the fatal club and failed to obliterate all the marks of the foul deed.

Immense was the excitement—so immense that Smith paid over the fifty to Captain Joe, shortly after breakfast, quietly, without asking any questions, and with a look that indicated his belief that the world was considerably smarter than he had once supposed it. All the boarders from all the houses rushed down to the scene of the tragedy. All the country people who heard of it (and they were hundreds in an hour or two) rushed in the same direction. The Coroner was sent for (no great distance, it is true) and arrived, though there was nobody (unfortunately) to inspect or "sit upon." Everybody talked murders of every kind, and this murder in particular. Poor Casey!—everybody said, especially those who had never known or cared about him. Captain Joe Darling, an old expert in the detection of crime, was called upon to examine the boat, the club, the blood and the hair, and gave it as his opinion that a fouller crime had never been committed. Victims were wanted by an enraged populace and an alarmed and horrified fifteen hundred of boarders. Had the terrible crimes of the city, then, really extended to the peaceful sea-shore? Was human life no longer safe anywhere? Two darkey waiters at one of the hotels, who had been off on a female darkey expedition the night before, and consequently could not give a very straight account of themselves, were strongly suspected of having satisfied some old grudge against poor Casey, and there was talk of lynching them. Finally a poor red-nosed toper who hung around Reed's, and who had once been heard to utter drunken hard words against Casey because he refused to treat, was arrested, examined before the Coroner, and seemcured in a fair way to take up his abode in Freehold jail, though everybody knew that he could neither row a boat nor commit any effectual violence on a child of ten years old. A reporter for one of the morning papers, who was down at the Branch on furlough and free board, started for the steamboat within half an hour after the discovery of the crime; and it was to his vigorous pen, enjoying for the moment the monopoly of an interesting subject—that the good people of this city were indebted for the paragraphs with startling headings which appeared in all the papers the same evening and the next morning: "Atrocious Murder at Long Branch! Great Excitement at the Boarding-Houses! Arrest of the Supposed Perpetrator!" etc., etc. An artist who happened to be on the spot, made drawings of the boat, the club, and as far as possible the blood and the hair, for one of the illustrated papers —which, strangely enough, never appeared, though they would have answered, quite as authentically as usual, for an illustration of a rape on shipboard or a snagged steamboat on the Mississippi.

Things were going on finely with the Long Branch murder, and it promised to blossom into proportions of great interest, when, at about two or three o'clock that afternoon, *before* the poor toper had been sent to Freehold, but *after* the reports had gone to the city and extended over the whole country—*Sim Casey made his appearance.* He did not seem much murdered, but in his usual health and spirits; though perhaps, owing to the easily acquired ten dollars, there may have been even *more* spirits than usual about him. He said he had gone down to Deal the evening before, to visit an old aunt who had been suddenly taken sick, and that he had been obliged to remain all night and till nearly noon. Of course he did not know anything about the situation of his boat—about the club, or the blood, or the hair.

Failing to discover anybody else missing (is that a Hibernicism?) the bottom suddenly fell out of the Long Branch murder; and nobody seemed disposed to acknowledge, even the next day, that they had seen or known anything about it. Perhaps there was a dim suspicion creeping through many heads, that somebody had been vended at a low figure. Perhaps there are people who believe that the hair came from the barber's at Long Branch Village, the blood from the butcher's, and the club from a neighboring wood-pile. Perhaps there are people who believe that Captain Joe, Lance and the Colonel perpetrated that murder and have not yet been punished! Who knows?

XII.

EDITORIAL PHRENOLOGY AT MIDNIGHT.

THE *Daily Hurryemup*, (that "busted" very soon after) was in apparently prosperous existence, and two of the editors and proprietors, with myself a sub, were waiting one night in the dingy little sanctum for proofs, which the foreman seemed determined to send us very slowly if at all. Wilkinson, the head of heads—the majesty of majesties, whose word was law after the rest of us had had our say, was a tall man with a pleasant but very grave face, before whom a stranger would about as soon have thought of cracking a joke as in the presence of the Khan of Tartary before dinner. He was really, meanwhile, a very jovial and jolly fellow, to those who fairly knew him, with a keen relish for a practical joke, and a closer insight into the tangled maze of politics than one man in ten thousand ever manages to attain. If he had another speciality, it was that of being the worst penman in the world, after Rufus Choate.

Boone, the second in command, better known as "Captain Boone," was a thick-set man of fifty, gray haired, with a round and jovial face a little marked by adventurous exposure—a good writer and a capital story-teller, whose specialty on the *Hurryemup* was to keep its commercial intelligence in order, and to write terrible stories about "Rats" and other amusing quadrupeds. Poor Charley Urquhart, best of dramatic critics and laziest of men, who sometimes made a quartette of our trio, had finished his labors for the night and gone home, escaping much more than he knew, besides missing something.

Bantering conversation had begun to lag, as midnight approached on the evening in question, and we were all growing tired of waiting for proofs (that the printers were doing anything up stairs!)—when relief from ennui unexpectedly arrived. The door opened, without warning from without, and a very seedy-looking personage entered, with a dilapidated bundle under his arm, and that general appearance graphically described as indicating "a gentleman and a scholar—a judge of liquor, and one who has seen better days." But seedy as the new-comer looked, he was evidently keen—keen as a briar, and his sharp face showed that he knew several things not set down on any popular chart of human conduct.

"Good evening, gentlemen! Hope I am not intruding on any privacy!" was the salutation of this strange customer; and then, without waiting for any reply, he went on at race-horse speed. "I am a phrenologist, gentlemen—a professor of the true art—none of your humbugs. Can beat Fowler and give him fifty points. Dig out the hidden bumps on any of your heads, quicker than a good dog can nose out a wood-chuck, or a politician get on the track of a fat office. Tell you what you can do, and what it is no use of your trying! Great science —phrenology! Any of you gentlemen like to have me go over his bumps and earn enough to get me supper and a bed?"

"How much do you charge for a thorough examination?" asked Wilkinson of the original, who had squatted himself uninvited in one of the vacant office-chairs, with the bundle on his lap, and was now drumming on both the arms of the chair with his unoccupied fingers.

"A quarter—only a quarter! Give you a splendid head for a quarter, and a re-mark-a-ble head for half a dollar, including chart," was the reply.

"Eh, what? Give a better character for a high price than a low one, do you?" asked the Captain.

"Certain-*ly*," said the stranger. "Publish any paid puffs in the *Hurryemup?*—I believe that is the name of your paper."

"Yes, that is the name," answered Wilkinson. "We do publish a few puffs. Why?"

"Give just as good a one for fifty cents as you do for fifty dollars? eh?" was the next interrogation.

"Not *quite*," said Captain Boone, laughing over the drollery of the illustration. "Suppose we take twenty-five cents worth apiece—eh, Wilkinson?"

"Just as you say," answered Wilkinson. "Of course *you* will take a chance, M——?"

"I'll bet he will!" said Boone. "Nobody ever heard of his backing out when he could talk about himself, or get talked about, for only a quarter!"

"You are the oldest, Captain—take your first chance!" said Wilkinson, as the itinerant phrenologist shoved back his cuffs and made a great flourish with his hands preparatory to commencement. The Captain took his seat in the big chair, which was to be the operating one; and the moment he had done so, when he thought that neither of us saw the movement, Wilkinson slipped behind, wrote a moment rapidly on a card and handed it to the operator, who, being behind the Captain, could also receive it without being noticed by the victim. There was such a thing as silver coin in the world in those days, (improbable as such an assertion may now seem to be,) and Wilkinson slipped a bright half-dollar into the dingy hand of the itinerant, with the card. That card contained—it is no matter how or when I discovered the fact—the following words: "Old sea-captain—tells infernal lies—thinks he can write—give him fits!" I could see that the quick eye of the phrenologist caught the words, and that he smiled. I could also see that he dropped the half-dollar into his pocket as if he had taken bribes before. He commenced operations on the Captain's head, tumbling his iron-gray hair about as if he had been about to shampoo him, while Wilkinson lit another of his everlasting segars and cocked up his feet on one of the desks.

"Fine head—remarkable head!" said the operator. "Capitally balanced. Intellectual organs predominate, of course, as they ought. Percepts fine—can see as far into a mill-stone as the next man. Animal organs only large enough to make a good family man. Destructiveness small—Combativeness middle size—Firmness much larger than usual. A fine head—a very fine head!"

I could see the Captain's face, in spite of the tumble of hair over it. It looked pleased and jubilant. Who of us is there that does not like flattery, even from a fool or a known impostor? Wilkinson's face did not look so well pleased. He probably had a momentary impression that he had lost his surreptitious half-dollar. Had he? We shall see!

"Inhabitativeness very small," the operator went on. "You could not possibly stay long in one place—must have been a great traveller, sir!"

"By George, he *does* know something about a head!" the flattered Captain could not avoid exclaiming. If he had a special point of pride greater than all others, it was in remembering how many thousands of miles of the earth's surface he had travelled over, by sea and land.

"Yes, he is evidently pretty well up!" said Wilkinson, drily, and at last perceiving that his leaven was beginning to work.

"But stop—good heavens!" said the phrenologist, pausing with a well-simulated appearance of horror. "What is this? I really hate to go on!"

"Why, what is the matter?" asked Captain Boone, suddenly brought down from his high-horse of self-gratulation. "Go on—what the d—l are you stopping for?"

"Well," said the intinerant, "I will go on if you wish, but I hope that you will not be offended at what I say. My art—the great art of phrenology—is always true, and I cannot falsify what it teaches."

Wilkinson was indulging in a quiet chuckle, which not only shook him but made the desk tremble; but he uttered no sound that the victim could hear. "Stop your d—lish nonsense and go on!" said the latter, once more, and the examination proceeded.

"I am sorry to say, sir," proceeded the wretch, "that Conscientiousness is totally wanting, and so is Continuity; and Marvellousness is very small—very small indeed. Without Continuity you can never write so that anybody will care to read what you have written ——."

"Ha! ha!" chuckled Wilkinson, this time loud enough to hear, but disguising the explosion under a feeble attempt at a cough.

"——It will be, in short, trash—dreadful trash!" went on the phrenologist.

"You scoundrel!" and the Captain made demonstrations of rising to punch the head of the man of science; but he was interrupted, and his purpose, if he had one, spoiled, by a clear, loud, ringing laugh from Wilkinson, who made no further attempt at disguise, but lay back in his chair and laughed until he was nearly black in the face.

"Ha! ha! ha! ha-h! ha-a-h!"

"Anything more?" asked the Captain, retaining his seat, but in that tone which says, louder than the words could convey it: "You cursed humbug and scoundrel! I should like to break your head if you were only worth the trouble!"

"Only a little more," said the operator. "Having Marvellousness so very small and lacking Conscientiousness altogether, you don't believe what any body tells you, nor what you say yourself; and if you should attempt to describe any of the things you had seen in your travels, you would—"

"Yes, that is what we want! out with it!" broke in Wilkinson, between two bursts of laughter.

"Yes, let us have the whole of it!" said Boone, with the air of a man who should have said: "It has rained pitchforks; now let the plough-shares come as soon as you like!"

"You would—that is—exaggerate."

"You mean, *lie*, I suppose!" queried the Captain.

"Yes, that is probably the better word," said the manipulator, and at about the same time the Captain "concluded his sitting" and made for the slanderer, who in turn made for the door. But the laugh of Wilkinson was too much for him, and before he could get ready to "execute judgment" on the wretch, he was obliged to join in the laughter, though with not the best grace in the world.

"A nice head!" said Wilkinson, when the explosion was over. "He *does* know something about heads, doesn't he?"

"Yes," answered the Captain, drily. "But let me see—yes, it is your turn now."

"I believe so," said Wilkinson, taking the chair in his turn. *He* was all right—the manipulator had received no hint as to *him*, and the tables could not possibly be turned! Perhaps if he could have heard the few words that I found time to say close in the ear of the operator, and the clink of the *two* half-dollars that fell into his pocket, conjoined with a punch in the Captain's side, he might have been a little less confident! The whispered words were about as pregnant as the card had been; "Death after all the women—makes love to all the lady contributors—close-fisted old hunks—thinks he is smart and everybody pulls the wool over his eyes—go it!"

He did "go it" with a vengeance!

"This is a very fine head," began the operator. (It was probably his stereotype commencement, as flattery is the first weapon of nearly all humbugs.) "You are a tall man, and, as is becoming, you have a long head."

"So has a donkey!" put in the Captain, parenthetically. He had assumed the chair just vacated by Wilkinson, his shorter legs not quite so far on the desk as his partner's had been, and sealing his recovered equanimity with a sandwich and a glass of old cider brought in by Tom from Mataran's. Wilkinson evidently heard the flattering remark, to judge by the sudden draw of his face; but he said nothing.

"As is not unusual with long heads," went on the operator, "the accumulative organs are well developed. Acquisitiveness is very large—seven plus—and as a consequence you hold your own. I should not like to say that you hold anything of other people's."

"Oh, you had better!" put in the subject, in a species of subterranean growl.

"But I hope there is no offence in my saying that a dollar sometimes looks, to your eyes, about the size of a carriage-wheel, and that—hem—that you don't need any blacksmith's vice to help you hold fast of it!"

"Bah!" said the victim—the only comment he deigned. (He was really a liberal man, and probably thought as much of his reputation in that direction, as in almost any other—*almost!*)

"But what have we here?" pursued the professional tormentor. "I find Combativeness very large, leading you to oppose nearly everybody in nearly everything." (Wilkinson *never* opposed any one, openly, when he could possibly avoid it.) "Then your percepts are low, and Marvellousness very large." (Wilkinson was as near to a skeptic in most regards as any man I have ever known, and prided himself on that quality.) "Consequently, though you may think yourself very keen, Self-esteem being six and a half, if you should attempt many transactions with people of the world, there would not be much difficulty in pulling the wool—"

"Down over his eyes!" the Captain concluded the sentence. "I say, Wilkinson, he *does* know something about a head, doesn't he? Always told you, you know, that you are nothing but a child, in *management.*"

Wilkinson did not reply a word. He had caught a glimpse by this time, I think, of the fact that he had been sold by one or the other of us, and his face was a study. No martyr on the rack or at the stake ever drew his face into queerer contortions, and yet no face ever expressed a more grim determination to go through with whatever might be coming. The examination went on. I saw the manipulator run his hand over the animal organs at the back of the head. Then, with a well-assumed expression of surprise, he stopped suddenly and withdrew his fingers. The Captain fetched a malicious nod and wink at me from his position behind the victim. The catastrophe was coming. Perfect silence for a moment, while the phrenologist stood with his fingers in the air as if he had burned them and was holding them up to cool.

"Well—what is the matter? Why in thunder don't you go on and get through?" broke out Wilkinson at length, half turning his head, when he found that the examination did not continue.

"I think—that is—I think I have gone far enough," said the manipulator, with a well-managed confusion. "There are some organs there that, that—"

"Yes, I think he had probably better stop," chuckled Captain Boone. "There are some secrets, you know, Wilkinson, that had better—"

"Go to the devil!" snarled the victim. "Look here, fellow!" to the operator, "if you don't go on and finish with my head, without any more outside comments, I'll finish *yours* with that big ruler yonder!" Wilkinson did not mean to have it said that he *dared* not have his whole head examined by any phrenologist living!

So adjured, the manipulator returned to his task.

"Well," he said, "you insist upon it, and I suppose I must earn my quarter. But really this is the most extraordinary thing I ever knew in my life. I hope you don't have any women coming around here!" (The *Hurryemup* office was the resort of half the literary women in town, and Wilkinson always the editor who received them.) "If so, I should advise their husbands always to come with them!"

"You would—would you?" gasped Wilkinson, on the very verge of being furious.

"Ho! ho! ho! ho! ho! ho-o-o-h-oh!" roared the Captain, with a long ringing termination to the last chuckle that showed exquisite enjoyment, and one that utterly defies spelling. He was eternally bantering Wilkinson about the number of women with whom he was closeted in his private room, and the latter always set up for St. Anthony, even to his most intimate friends.

"With Continuity only two and the most extraordinary bump of Amativeness I ever felt, I should think that you would make love to every woman you saw, old or young, and that you would never stick to any one for more than two hours. An extraordinary head for love-making, sir, but a dangerous one, I should say! Your wife had better look out for the servant-girls! That is all, sir!"

"That is all, is it?" said Wilkinson, springing from his chair with a "Heugh!" of relief like that which expresses the throwing off of some terrible incubus. "That is all, is it? Well, I should say it was quite enough! Get out of here, you scoundrel, or I'll—"

"Oh, no, you won't; Wilkinson!" said the Captain, just concluding another of those stentorian bursts of laughter that only solid men can manage. "You only gave the fellow fifty cents to ruin *my* character for life, and he had a dollar to destroy *yours*."

"Ha! ha! ha! ho! ho! ho!" roared both the partners in concert at this development, while I believe I joined them, and I am very sure that the itinerant phrenologist looked as proud as if he had won the great success of his life. So he had—made two dollars and twenty-five cents in less than an hour, at midnight—enough to buy him not only supper and lodging, but to keep him on a very respectable "drunk" for at least half a week,—besides the privilege of handling familiarly three of the most extraordinary heads of the century!

Modesty forbids me to mention all the developements which came out when the two previous victims set the tormenter at *my* head. I have a dim recollection that he found a hole where Veneration should have been—that he declared himself unable to measure Alimentiveness, (*i. e.*, gluttony)—found Firmness (*i. e.*, stubbornness) eleven, and Self-esteem fourteen (seven and a half being the top of the scale) —that he found Language prominent enough to make me a gabbler, and Caution large enough to make me a coward—and that he discovered such a sad deficiency in Amativeness and all the corresponding organs, that I resolved never to speak to a woman from that time forward. I think I did not enjoy that examination quite as much as I had done the two preceding; but Wilkinson and Captain Boone had laughter enough over it to salve their own wounds, and what more was wanted?

I wonder if either of the two remembers, as well as myself, that jolliest illustration phrenology ever had in this city—over three editorial craniums at midnight, in the dingy sanctum of the now long defunct *Daily Hurryemup!*

XIII.

MY LAST SUNDAY ON SKATES.

Some twenty or twenty-five years have elapsed since I of this writing tempted the slippery skate. The world has grown very much older in that quarter of a century; and I have grown older with it, in spite of all the "Elixir of Youth" I have been able to extract from a good appetite and a laughing disposition. I very well remember the last essay, and the memory alone would be quiet sufficient to drive off temptation when it appeared in the shape of the double serpent of the strap, runner and buckle.

Sundry essays made at an earlier period had not developed immense capabilities for keeping the perpendicular and emulating the speed of the wind, when mounted on the grooved rails which accompany the rolling-stock instead of being run over by it; and obtaining eventual possession of a better and bigger pair of skates, I did incontinently practise all the art and mystery of the profession, surreptitiously, during two or three weeks of one hard winter, on a little patch of ice about four feet by six, surrounded by clumps of alders, in a swamp so sheltered that no eyes but those of the wondering birds and rabbits would be likely to take note of any misfortune. There I went through the innumerable phases of the slip, the slide, the fall, the tumble, the bump, the crash which showed stars, the forward fall which abraded the nose and dilapidated the knees of the trowsers, and all the other ills to which awkward beginners on skates are immediately subject.

At the end of this period, having advanced as far in the art and mystery of skating as the Prince Regent of England had in fiddling, when he got so that he "couldn't fiddle at all"—I determined upon an essay upon a broader field. This, in the neighborhood, could only be secured upon the mill-pond; and during all the week days it was occupied by relays of boys who seemed to have grown into the use of skates as naturally as they had come into their ragged trowsers, and without a particle of sympathy for the slides and tumbles of less versatile humanity. To make a first essay on the broad field before *them*, would never do, and Sunday was the only holiday of the ice-pond. (Let it be remembered that a quarter of a century ago Sunday was less of a day of recreation than at present, and that in Puritan neighborhoods it was scarcely used at all for the amusements then held to be altogether secular.) On that day the troublesome demons of the skate would all be kept at home or packed off to Sunday-school and meeting, and I should be as much alone and as independent as Robinson Crusoe on his desert island before he had found ever a Man-Friday.

Well, to that spot, immediately after the hastily-swallowed Sunday dinner, I wended, skates under my arm and expectation up to several degrees beyond the moral Fahrenheit. Clear, cool and delicious was the afternoon, and calm, placid and shining lay the surface of the pond, on which such alluring mathematical figures were before long to be described. The old mill, with its planks extending out over the ice, lay lonely and deserted, and the logs that formed a border around it were among the most harmless of spectators. Not a human being in sight, and not even one of the winter flights of crows sailing overhead to make the bashful debutant nervous.

Down on the bank at the edge of the pond I knelt, and strapped on those skates as skates had never been strapped on before. Up I rose, and proceeded to make the first grand "strike out" of the occasion. Horror!—the first foot had scarcely gone twelve inches on its mission, when I caught sight of a human face and figure! Poets and philosophers may rave as they will about "the human face divine," but there are times when the human face is, to the man who sees it when he has no propensity to see it, very nearly infernal! Two tigers and a wild cat could not have been so unwelcome at that juncture, as anything wearing a hat and pantaloons, not to mention the possessor of a bonnet in fee simple. But there was a face, and casting a horrified glance towards it, not quite enough attention was paid to the ice ahead and the retention of the perpendicular, and down somebody came with a crash that made the old alder woods ring for a quarter of a mile.

"Capital! go it! try it again!" chuckled a voice, and arising with all the physical agility which was then a prominent feature in my character, as modesty now is,—I discovered Jake Jerolamon, proprietor of the mill, seated on the end of the planks overhanging the pond, half a white-pine board in one hand and a quarter-of-a pound lump of chalk in the other.

"What in thunder are you doing there?" I ejaculated, skating clumsily towards him, though without any "attraction" except a "passional" one not recognized by the free-lovers.

"Doing here? why *sitting* here!" answered Jake, in the coolest and most provoking of tones possible. He was well-known over the entire section as one of the most merciless of wags and practical-jokers, and no other ten men could have inspired as much dread under the circumstances.

"Jake Jerolamon, you had better go home, where you belong!" was the ungracious reply. "But what are you going to do with that board and chalk?"

"Keep an account of the number of times you fall!" was the assuring answer. "See, there's one of them down already! If I can't get 'em all on the two sides of the board, why I'll get a ladder and fill up the side of the mill!"

"You will, eh?" said I, raging impotently.

"Yes," said Jerolamon, in the same drawling and bantering tone. "I shall stay here for a while to keep 'count for you, and then be ready to pull you out when you fall in."

"The d——l you will!" said I, irreverently. "Now look here, Jake Jerolamon—"

"Oh, I know what you are going to say," interrupted Jake. "You dare not skate before anybody, and so you are going to pull off your skates and go home, on purpose to disappoint me."

Cruel Jake!—if he had sounded the whole depth of human nature he could not have hit upon a more certain means to induce me to remain and be laughed at and mangled.

"You think so, do you!" said I, viciously, and determined not to be driven off. "That is just where you are wrong. I am going to skate here all the afternoon."

"Oh, then I shall go and get another board,"

said Jake, rising. "Here, girls you may as well come out, for the thing is all settled."

And out of the little office of the mill popped Susan and Kate Jerolamon, Jake's daughters, rosy, saucy and laughing, and a city cousin with them, whom I had been trying to engage in a flirtation any time within the last month! By what witchcraft Jake had known that I was going to skate on the mill-pond, and brought them there, there was no means of knowing; but there was a pretty situation for a bashful man and a bad skater—no, no skater at all!

Of course I should have run away if I could, but I could not. There was just enough contrariness of disposition to prevent *that.* Then the girls insisted that I should skate, and *could* skate, they *knew* I could!—and whether they were ridiculing me or not was of no manner of consequence. So while old Jake used his chalk and his board, and the three girls sat ranged upon the plank like so many lighter-colored crows on a fence—*I skated.*

There are moments in every man's life, I fancy, so full of unutterable horror that the curtain should be drawn between them and the eye of common humanity; and my special horror is that two hours of skating under quadruple supervision. Afraid to go off and ashamed to go on—applauded alike when a moderate success had been achieved and when a bad fall had been accomplished—coming down about twice in a minute during one hundred and twenty revolutions of that period—head aching and temples throbbing, and with a worse pain at the heart than in any other portion of the animal economy—bruised to a pumice and stiffened till neither arms nor legs could be lifted without violent effort—all my falls relentlessly set down on the white pine board by Jake Jerolamon's ruthless fingers, and all timed by the merry laughter of three mischievous girls who had never learned the name, much less the quality of mercy,—I submit that I had on that particular afternoon quite skating enough to last for a quarter of a century!

So far as I can remember at this distance of time, it was rather a relief when the catastrophe was reached by my skating over the brook or channel of the pond, (which was never thoroughly frozen,) falling in that opportune place, and going in up to the arm-pits, to be dragged out by old Jake with a pole and sent home shivering, under an assurance from Jerolamon that he would save the board, and a peal of laughter from the girls that capped the climax of mortification.

That is my last skating-adventure, so far, in spite of all the temptations of Central Park ponds and even all the added attractions of Brooklyn and Jersey City. Have I not had good cause to be shy?—answer, athletic youths in the short coats and skating-caps, and sprightly young ladies *avec les jolies jambes*, who have almost forgotten dancing for the healthier out-door exercise?

XIV.

THE GREAT SHORTPORT BURGLARY.

It was about the time that the debatable ground between the City of New-York and the country forty or fifty miles distant, began to be hunted over by the burglars, and when short paragraphs on the subject had assumed some frequency in the country papers, that I was for the time a resident of Shortport, a maritime village lying not quite a hundred miles from the great city, and where great sensations were got up on a small capital, with as much facility as I have ever seen displayed in any other operation of society. It had innumerable great events while honored with my residence, but I suspect that none of them made so abiding an impression as *the* burglary.

It came about in this wise:

Shortport was not only one of the great molluscular depôts, from which the great city drew a large proportion of the delicious bivalves consumed by the million in its saloons and restaurants, but the entrépôt of a steamboat line by which there was a daily communication with the modern Babylon. It was consequently known to be easily accessible to any dangerous characters who might be disposed to profitable rustication; and only a few weeks before the particular period of which I write, Middleport, a town at a few miles distance, had been visited during the night by a couple of real burglars, armed with all the portable tools of the fraternity, and almost robbed.

I say *almost*—for it happened in that particular case that one of the respectable youthful citizens of that flourishing community, returning home late from what is commonly called a "spark," came upon the industrious personages who were prying open a door or two; and they went out of town, one of them in the constable's cart, and the other with lead enough in him to keep him from swimming to advantage.

Of course burglars were spoken for, then, for every village in the county; and it was rumored that all the horse-pistols which had been lying idle since the time when our sea-coast was threatened by Cockburn in the last war, were cleaned up and loaded, and a few cheap revolvers added to them. Of course all that large class of the female community, who had been for years "looking for the boots under the bed" without being able to find them, took up the cry; and innumerable cups of tea and some snuff fell a sacrifice to the "strong necessity of" discussing the prevailing topic. But for a few weeks no burglars appeared any where in the section.

At length, one very dark night in early November, Captain Howell, who had happened to be detained over late at his coasting schooner on the Bay, was coming up Main street, about half-past twelve, and was startled by a light in front of one of the fancy stores on the street. He stopped—there they were, sure! Fortunately the Captain had on india-rubber boots, the waterman's indispensable companions, and was enabled to approach without making a great deal of noise. He was bound to have them, single-handed and unarmed though he might be, against no one knew how many desperate fellows, and he crept up noiselessly.

Nearer and nearer, and there they were, sure enough. Three of them, and the tallest a man of not less than six feet and a half, engaged at that very moment in fumbling close by the door. One of the two others, both shorter men, was holding a dark lantern that threw a dim and doubtful ray on all their faces, and the Captain saw that they were an ill-looking set of fellows indeed. Three, and one of them of such a size—the prospect of contending with them single-handed was a bad one, and the Captain decided that there was no use in risking his life so rashly. He would give them a wide berth, as they say at sea, but go near enough to see their faces plainly, so that the constable might know better how to pursue them the next day. And so he went up closer.

"Hark!" the Captain's foot struck an old piece of tin or iron, and quick as thought the slide of the dark lantern was shut and all was darkness. He went on up the path, then, and the burglars were not in it. They had of course been alarmed, and decamped, probably for the night. So the Captain went home and to bed; but he had slept better in the Gulf Stream, with his little hooker laid-to in a storm, than that night, albeit it was late.

The next morning was one of excitement in Shortport. Of course Captain Howell considered it his duty to give warning of the probable fact that burglars were "bobbin' around," and he did so. Then it became apparent that they had been heard that night at more places than one. At Wilson's at about half-past eleven, there had been a noise at the front gate; at Smith's the door was shaken two or three times, Mrs. Smith thought *then*, about midnight; at Jones', men were heard walking around the house all night, and Mrs. Jones "hadn't slept a wink, but she'd no thought of their being burglars, or she wouldn't have been abed at all, that she wouldn't!" At Porter's one of the shutters of the shop was found open in the morning; and around pretty much every house in the centre of the town there were found plenty of footmarks.

Truly it was a mercy that in all these attempts the fellows had not succeeded in making an entrance anywhere. But unquestionably they had thought it unsafe after being seen by Howell, to make any further attempts that night, and were holding back for the next.

The next night—aye! there was the rub. The next night was, evidently, to witness a general descent by a body of burglars, armed with skeleton keys, jimmies, chisels, priers, &c., on devoted Shortport; and the consternation was general. The town had no regularly organized police, and only occasionally indulged in a body of that description as amateurs, when there was a row to be quelled or made. But it was judged best to have one for this occasion; so half a dozen were promptly organized as a central force, and posted at nine o'clock in Wiggins' warehouse, while a dozen others were to act as patrols in different parts of the town. The principal arms of the central body were a box of cigars, two pitch-forks, one hand-saw, one horse-pistol, and a pile of bricks at the door. The patrols were variously accoutred with canes, two pistols, one table-knife, (large size) heavy soled boots, and fists of great power; so that the burglars, if discovered, were likely to suffer badly.

But while this was going on in the public way, privately there was a like preparation. A., who was notoriously nervous and kept batchelor's hall, made arrangements for letting things rip and keeping out of harm's way, by removing his bed into a side closet, and taking everything in with him, except the stove, which would not go through the door.

B. was a man of considerable wealth, and did not like to trust outside watching; and at the same time he couldn't possibly convey all his valuables into his bed room. So he had a camp-bed fixed up in the parlor, and arranged himself to lie awake all night, looking at the gilt clock on the mantel, and listening for a scratch at the key-hole. Of course he went to sleep in half an hour, and the seven thunders would not have woken him.

Mrs. C. had always been great on tins. Tin pans, large, small, very small, cups, dishes and platters, graced her kitchen shelves; and no one had ever been able to see what she wanted of so many, for her small family. But now the use came out. She was enabled to pile a tin pyramid exactly to the top of her only outside door, so that if the burglars did come in they would come with a smash, and probably be frightened out of doing any damage.

Mrs. D. provided herself, (her husband was away) early in the evening, with the wood-pile axe, to take to bed with her. Unfortunately on going to bed she forgot it down stairs and lay awake all night wishing that she dare go down to get it.

E. went away on a voyage during the afternoon. His wife cried, and prophesied that they would all be robbed and murdered before he came back; but he recommended going to bed early, and putting her head under the bed-clothes, so that if any damage was done she wouldn't hear it. She thought him very unfeeling, but he went away apparently very little alarmed, to general wonder.

And so on to the end of the chapter. Never was village so on the *qui vive* as Shortport. Never had burglars such a look for a reception, as at that particular place and on that occasion. But, could it be believed? the burglars didn't come. Not a stir in the streets, not an attempt at a door or a window. Could they have heard of the preparations?—Strange!

Yes, very strange; but not quite so much so when it accidentally leaked out on the morning after, that *the burglars seen by Captain Howell were three very good fellows belonging to the village, and E., one of them, with an old lantern from one of the stables, posting political handbills prior to election.* They had heard the Captain coming, concluded to "sell" him by blowing out the light, dodged home, and kept their own counsel long enough to scare Shortport into fits.

My own impression is that afterwards, any time during the next six months, burglars might really have done a good business in the village, for half a dozen persons might have been seen prying open all the shutters in town, and would only have been suspected of playing another practical joke. And if any one risked using the word "burglary," anywhere within the confines of Shortport, during the same period, it was necessary to do so when the door was open and there was a clear field for escaping the broom-handles, smoothing-irons and other missiles that were very likely to follow the impertinence.

XV.

EXTRA DRUMMING AT THE OLD BROADWAY.

I do not remember what they were playing at the Broadway Theatre on a night which recalls itself to my memory; but it is a matter of not the least consequence. I know that the season was that in which the Ronzani ballet-troupe made their first appearance in this country, and when Louise Lamoureux was for the time the star of the ballet.

Strolling into the house one evening, and going forward to one of the front benches of the parquette, I stumbled upon my (and everybody's) old friend, Dr. Melton McPenzie, then just closing a connection with one of the New York journals, and on the point of going to Philadelphia to assume the still more influential position which he has held from that time to the present.

Dr. Mac was in about as jolly and satisfactory a humor as usual, and we chatted, of course, while the curtain was down after the first act, of newspapers, theatrical affairs and everything else imaginable. Some of the members of the orchestra were in their seats, though part of them, and among the rest old John Cooke, who wielded the baton, had gone out for a sandwich or something less solid.

Suddenly I saw the Doctor's face light up with a recognition, and he said, looking towards the orchestra:

"Ah, there is a man I once knew, though I have not met him for a long time. I must speak to him a few moments. Come over and see him—you will find him worth knowing."

We left our seats and crossed to the right of the orchestra railing, within which sat the man he had noticed. He had the big bass-drum beside him and a smaller one and two kettle-drums in the immediate neighborhood, and was, in fact, Robinson, the drummer of the orchestra. The Doctor and the musician greeted each other as old acquaintances, and the former introduced me. I noticed that Robinson seemed a bit of an original, and decidedly odd, with a strong propensity for keeping a straight face under circumstances in which any one else would have laughed. McPenzie and he had been old acquaintances in the old country, and had not previously met for years; so during the long *entr' acte* of a show-piece with much set machinery, they had many things to chat about, the Doctor and myself leaning over the railing.

With the usual propensity of very busy people for doing what I had no business to do, I leaned over and hit the big bass-drum a few slight thumps with my fingers, making the burly instrument growl a few notes away down in its intestines.

"Hush! sh!" said the Doctor. "Not quite so loud, please. Old Cooke may hear you, and then—"

"Well, let him hear!" said Robinson. "*He* won't hurt anything! *I'm* drummer here, not Cooke."

"By the way," said the Doctor, "you ought by this time to have been something more than a drummer, Robinson."

"Heigho! I suppose so!" was the answer, in a tone so doubtful that I did not know if he cared whether he wielded a baton or a drumstick.

"If it is not quite so high a walk of music as playing some of the other instruments, drumming is at least *easier* than most of the others, I suppose," I said.

"Oh yes," answered Robinson—"easy enough; in fact, almost too easy. There is not a drummer in any orchestra in the world, who would not rather play more of the time than he is called to do by the score."

"Humph!" said the Doctor. "They ought to write a few pieces especially for the drummer—a few good long pieces that would require him to beat all the time."

"Or," I said, "perhaps it would answer the purpose if the drummer should beat all the way through a piece already written. I suppose *that* would kick up a little confusion, wouldn't it?"

"A *little*," said Robinson, drily.

"Eh?" broke in the Doctor, his eye flashing with a sudden droll idea—"by George, I never thought of that before! Why not, Robinson?"

"What?" asked Robinson—"beat through the whole of some composition, without any regard to the score?"

"Yes," said the Doctor. "Why not?"

"Here?" asked Robinson.

"Yes, here and now!" answered the Doctor, who had just got fairly on the trail of a gigantic mischief. "What do you play next?"

Robinson looked at the books, and I think that the next piece to be played was something of Mozart's, of considerable length. At all events it was one of the pet compositions of one of the learned

German composers, full of delicate passages and fine effects in musical light and shade.

"Yes," said the Doctor—"that will do capitally. When old Cooke comes in, just go through that whole piece like a house a-fire. Don't stop for anybody or anything!"

"Humph!" said Robinson, "I suppose you know that such a spree would cost me my place in the orchestra; if it did not prevent my ever getting another."

"Well," said the Doctor, "all I can say is, go ahead with it. Don't flinch or falter, and put in the licks as if you were drumming for a big army on the march. You know *me*, Robinson, don't you?"

"I do," said Robinson, "thoroughly."

"And you believe that what I promise I will do?"

"Yes," said Robinson, "without a doubt."

"Then," said the Doctor, "I promise you that if this little job of drumming on your own hook costs you your place, you shall have a better one within twenty-four hours. And here," drawing out a bill and handing it out to Robinson—"here is an X to pay you for your trouble. Dare you go it?"

"I *dare* do any thing," said Robinson, "and I *think* that I could manage to keep a straight face through the operation. I will—yes, I will do it; and remember your promise if it gets me into a scrape! Get back among the audience where I cannot see you, or you may make me laugh. Here comes Cooke—now for one satisfactory drum, if I never have another!"

Cooke came in with the balance of his orchestra, at the moment, and the curtain being almost ready to rise after the long *entr' acte*, the conductor took his fiddle and bow. Doctor McPenzie and myself went back a few seats, where we could see not only the orchestra but most of the audience, and where we could be at the same time out of the way of Robinson. With excellent judgment, that worthy did not begin too soon. Cooke waved his fiddle-bow and the interlude commenced in a passage of rare beauty and delicacy. Gradually this swelled higher and the chorus came in; and after a time there were two or three clashes for the cymbals, followed by a dozen taps for the drum. Here the new model musician began. Robinson gave the taps of the drum correctly but decidedly. A little further on was a cornet solo. As this was reached all the other instruments fell off, except a single violoncello which was to furnish the accompaniment.

All the other instruments, of course, *except* Robinson's bass-drum. That pounded along, regularly and determinedly, when the cornet solo commenced; and that pounded along, regularly and solemnly, when it finished. Cooke looked around, when he found the drum did not rest—his face expressive of the blankest astonishment and then of the most absolute disgust. He motioned peremptorily to Robinson to stop, with his fiddle-bow, but that worthy was looking another way, with the gravest of faces, and did not see him. At about this time occurred a passage of complicated harmonies, and the attention of the conductor was necessarily absorbed in managing the different elements, though he must have heard the drum still banging away.

This harmonic passage over, occurred one loud and stormy, in which the cymbals and the drum again came into play. This gave Robinson an excuse to redouble the force of his blows, and they began to fall on the hide of the drum-head as if the drummer had been paid for his music by the pound. Heavily as the instruments crashed, and fierce as were the blasts of the horns, Robinson's drum thundered out clearly above them all. Two or three times Cooke managed to look around to see what could be the matter, and once he shook his fiddle-bow threateningly at the delinquent, who might at that moment have been surveying land-claims on the steppes of Siberia, for any attention he paid the *maestro*.

By this time the audience had begun to notice the fidget of the conductor and the wondering looks of some of the other performers; and by this time, too, they had begun to realize that a drum thundering through all the finer passages of an intricate composition (solos and all) was something of a novelty. Some began to laugh, and a few clapped hands. This encouraged Robinson, who banged away harder than ever, with a regularity to which the efforts of the "conscientious man" in the chorus of the Academy of Music, are fitful and nervous.

At length the composition ran into what was intended to be a delicate allegro, with the violins tinkling and one or two flutes just breathing the suspicion of a sound. What it was intended to be, was one thing; what it was on this occasion, was quite another. A little diminished in the force of the blows, perhaps, but still regular and heavy enough to dwarf all the other sounds, came the "tap-tap" "boom-boom" of Robinson's drum. It was only at a rare interval that the "tinkle-tinkle" of a violin or the "toot-toot" of a flute could be distinguished. By this time the audience began to enjoy the joke pretty generally, and the clapping of hands increased. By this time, too, most of the orchestra had got so full of laughter, that they could scarcely play at all, though they managed not to break down. By this time, finally, poor Cooke's face had grown to be the oddest mixture any man ever saw. Astonishment—rage—vexation—undecision what to do—all were ludicrously blended there, and making *him*, altogether, a little funnier yet than Robinson with his steady work and his grave face.

As the piece came very near its close, the old man could stand it no longer. He sprung to his feet, jerked his fiddle-bow up in the air with an angry motion, and yelled out at the top of his voice "Stop!" He might as well have told Niagara to stop thundering. All the orchestra were now fairly carried away by the joke, and every man blew, and fiddled, and crashed, with all the power of the instrument he happened to have in hand. Robinson's blows on the drum continued as regular as ever, but they had become fearful in their ponderosity. Every moment I expected to see the head of the drum go in and his efforts come to an untimely end.

The din grew maddening. Half the audience were laughing, or clapping, and one third of them were on their feet in uncontrollable enjoyment. The Doctor had laughed off and lost his spectacles, and I had bargained for a pain in the side for a week. A little fellow in the corner of the orchestra, who had been playing some minor instrument, suddenly came to the conclusion that he was not making noise enough, and pitched for the kettle-drum, on which he volunteered a "rat-tat-a-tat" accompaniment loud enough to have answered for a charge of cavalry. Poor old Cooke could stand it no-longer. He made one more attempt to spring up and stop the torrent; but if he spoke his voice was drowned like a whisper beside a frog-pond in full blast. He cast one despairing look at the audience and orchestra—clapped his hands to his ears as if to shut out the echoes of Pandemonium—then dropped fiddle and bow and plunged through the door under the stage, and disappeared.

He was scarcely gone when the interlude came

to a conclusion, every man doing his best to the very last, and the final bangs of Robinson's drum sounding above the crash as distinctly as if he had been playing altogether alone. Such a storm of shouts and clappings of applause, followed by three such cheers, as those that saluted the daring innovator when the performance was over, I think never burst through the dome of any theatre before or since. And such a grave, stately and self-satisfied bow as Robinson rose and made in acknowledgement, has not often been seen even when a political General was called out at the Academy or Wallack's. The thing was a grand success, and no doubt the performers saw it in that light, though it is to be doubted whether Cooke, flying away from that outrage upon all music, took precisely the same view of it!

I am sorry that I do not know the after result of the affair, and its effect on the fortunes of Robinson—but I do not. Any one who wishes to ascertain, may do as I expect to do some day, after this reminder — drop into the snugly crowded little library of Dr. Melton McPenzie, in Philadelphia, and ask him between two puffs of the Orleans-Galignani meerschaum.

XVI.

THE TWO-FORTY FUNERAL.

A LITTLE paragraph went the rounds of the papers a few weeks ago, relating how one Spurr, keeper of a livery stable, had grown so much in the habit of cautioning his customers not to drive his horses very fast—that one day when one of them came after a horse and carriage to attend a funeral, Spurr gave the customary caution: "Mind that you don't drive fast!" "I shall drive fast enough to keep up with the procession," replied the customer, "even if I kill the horse!"

It does not seem a very difficult thing, generally, to keep up with a funeral procession, on its way to the place of burial, however the hired carriages come *back* from Greenwood or Calvary Cemetery on the hurry-skurry, as if they had been attending any thing else rather than the deposit of the human body in the place of its last repose. But I have known one instance, at least, where good stock and sharp driving were necessary to keep up with the procession when on the way to the grave; and that is the circumstance I am about to relate.

Two events were to occur on the same day, at and near the little village of Edgewood, then the place honored by the residence of the writer. Two more dissimilar events could not have been thrown together, by any possibility; and yet each demanded the presence of a minister, and according to usual consent each demanded the presence of a considerable number of people. Captain Bob Hollis, master-mariner in the merchant service, was to be married; and Uncle Ben Robinson, a venerable citizen of eighty, was to be buried. The marriage of Captain Bob was set for ten o'clock in the morning, to be followed by a breakfast, which was really a dinner, eaten at such a time as to allow Captain Bob and his bride to reach the next station, and catch the noon train for their bridal tour; and Uncle Ben was to have his funeral sermon preached at twelve, at the little church of Edgewood, and be afterwards interred in a cemetery at several miles distance.

Captain Bob was a man in very easy circumstances, owning one of the finest houses in the neighborhood. He had been several years a widower, before making up his mind to his second marriage; and the lady who was about to plight her faith to him had been the reigning belle of the section for more years than the Captain had been maintaining his state of celibacy. Add to these facts the additional one that Captain Bob had been pretty well known as a boon companion, and connected in business, first or last, with nearly all the first residents; and it may be supposed that such an event as his wedding could not be allowed to come off without invitations being extended to all the "first citizens."

Unfortunately there is sometimes a difference of opinion as to what constitutes a "first citizen," between persons estimated and those who have the duty of estimating them. No one is quite satisfied that he has been taken at his full worth, except when he is called upon to pay his tax, at which latter time he has no idea that he has been depreciated. Edgewood had one specimen of the outraged and the down-trodden. He was a good-looking little fellow enough, physically, except that high-living and indolence had given him more—well, we will call it *embonpoint*—than the law of gracefulness allows,—and that the spiteful envy and jealousy of his disposition had made him as grey as a Norway rat, long before he should have sported one thread of silver. He had once commanded in a "slab" militia regiment, and had there attained the rank of Major, which he took as good care that all who addressed him should use before his surname, as he did that his boot-heels (he was by occupation a cobbler) should be sufficiently high to add an inch to his stature, and that he should always strut with his head well up and his paunch well stuck forward.

Major Jeff Taddlewick, once as poor as Job's proverbial turkey, had during the few years preceding acquired some property through the deaths of relatives, and in certain petty land-speculations; and he fell into the very common error of supposing that he had been meanwhile accumulating a corresponding amount of additional respectability. Nothing could have been further from the fact; for every dollar had added to his arrogance and pomposity, while increasing occupation had done nothing to wean him from his habit of poking his Roman nose into the business of every one with whom he could manage to force himself into contact.

Careful people ceased talking, even if engaged in the most harmless discussions, the moment that Major Taddlewick's nose was seen entering the door—from the certainty that if they continued, within an hour some totally different version of the conversation would be circulated in the street, and the materials for several quarrels scattered among the community. Gayer and more reckless people, who did not care for results, tolerated the Major's company and rather enjoyed it, for he had a sediment of drollery at the bottom of his ill-nature, which would have made him a pleasant companion had the black fang of envy been extracted from his mental mouth. He had the faculty of practical joking, too, and sometimes made a hit with it, though his malicious and reckless disposition generally managed to get a good joke into a wrong place and do more or less injury by it.

Major Taddlewick had heard the day before, that a good many invitations were out for Captain Bob's wedding, and he had received an insult of the gravest character in Captain Bob's failure to invite him and Mrs. Major Taddlewick. Revenge on the Captain and all his guests became a matter of necessity. This he brought about in a manner peculiarly his own, the catastrope already foreshadowed being the result. Of course the key to the mystery was not obtained until long after, and I only came into possession of it by a very roundabout course of procedure; but the explanation must here be given before the event itself.

There is perhaps no class of the community so thoroughly versed in all the properties of plants and herbs, as the old darkey womn who yet exist in some portions of the country, and who have brought their knowledge from the African coast or the West Indies, where it has originated in the infernal operations of the "Obii" or charms, in which everything, from the rankest root that grows in the field to the thigh-bone of a new-born baby, is brought occasionally into requisition.

Not far from the little village of Edgewood lived Aunt Sarah, a darkey woman of sixty-five or seventy years, black as the ace of spades, withered like an oak-leaf in November, the dispenser of cake and beer to a wide circle of small boys who took occasion to pass the lane where her little hut was located, an unexceptionable cook, and employed as an assistant at almost all the "great occasions" that took place in the locality.

It came into the knowledge of Major Taddlewick, that the old woman was retained as assistant cook and waiter for the great occasion at Captain Bob's; and within an hour afterwards—to wit, on the evening before the wedding, he paid a visit to Aunt Sarah's hovel. Exactly what words passed no one can say, or how high was the bribe the Major offered; but certain it is that the old woman agreed to apply her knowledge of aperient and laxative herbs that would "physic" without endangering life, and to "doctor" the principal articles of food at the wedding breakfast, with such tasteless preparations as would create no suspicion at the time but a good deal of *certainty* afterwards.

Well, the eventful day arrived, big with the marital fate of Captain Bob Hollis and the mortuary fate of Uncle Ben Robinson. A fine clear bracing day in autumn it was, especially fitted for a "turn out" at either or both the "festivities." Carriage after carriage rolled up to Captain Bob's, Domine Stanton's one-horse fly among the rest, and the yards and grounds and the edge of the wood adjoining were soon crowded with vehicles.

Unfortunately, as I thought at the time, but fortunately, as I thought not long afterwards, I was among the number of the "slighted," like Major Jeff Taddlewick. But I had plenty of parole information of the beauty of the bride, the resplendent face of Captain Bob, the benevolent pomposity of Domine Stanton, the motherly smirk of Mrs. Domine Stanton (who considered herself a *little* the better half in the pastoral charge), the profuse display of hot meats, poultries and pastries at that breakfast which was really a dinner, and all the other acts and things appertaining to the joyous occasion.

Suffice it to say that the wedding festivities ended, the new married couple drove away to the station, and the wedding party, forgetting the wedding suite and drawing their faces down to the appropriate length for such an occasion, one by one drove down to the little church to attend the obsequies of Uncle Ben Robinson. At that part of the day's occupation, which did not need an invitation, I was present, as also at the funeral progress which followed.

I could have sworn, two or three times during the funeral sermon, that Domine Stanton was not entirely at ease, and more than once I noticed symptoms of uneasiness and some indecorous going out on the part of the congregation. All this was a mystery, but excited little comment.

The funeral services were finally over, the body in the hearse, and the procession moving towards the little cemetery. I was in one of the carriages that followed the mourners closest, and consequently did not have any opportunity of observing the train behind, but had the carriage of Domine Stanton, who preceded the Doctor and the hearse, in full view. We had a long closed lane to traverse, over an entirely open reach of country, with scarcely a tree or hedge to break the prospect for miles. At the end of that distance, and in the neighborhood of the cemetery to which we were proceeding, a range of thick woods on an open common bounded the prospect.

We had perhaps traveled two or three miles, when I observed with surprise that Domine Stanton broke suddenly away from the procession and drove rapidly ahead in the direction of the cemetery. I supposed he had some directions to give in advance of the arrival of the cortege, and explained the singular movement in that manner. A moment after, a pair of spanking bays came by at a full trot, with a load that I had seen at the church. At this I really *did* begin to wonder; and that wonder rapidly increased as another carriage broke out of the line and shot by at the full trotting speed of the horses.

Another and still another, and each seemed to be going faster than the other. By this time my companion and myself (he had not been at the wedding,) became satisfied that something remarkable must have occurred, and we drew our light carriage to the side of the road, for safety from the heavier vehicles. Still another and then another came at increased speed, and directly one carriage containing half a dozen ladies and gentlemen, went by on a full run, the driver plying his lash as if he was escaping from a pack of prairie-wolves or hyenas.

By this time we of the stationary vehicle had made up our minds that something involving life or death must certainly have occurred before or behind, and this idea was not lessened when we saw the driver of the hearse (who *had* been at the wedding,) break off from his sober gait, ply the lash to his horses, and away with the most rapid of the flying squadron.

Perhaps half-a-dozen carriages were left slowly jogging along or stationary with wonder; but all the rest, apparently in less time than I have taken to tell it, were flying away on what appeared to be a race for life. What they *were* flying for, and that the strip of woods was the destination upon which all had suddenly agreed, all my readers may imagine. But they cannot imagine the scene—especially after the hearse got fairly into motion; and such a funeral gait was never struck before, I venture to affirm, since the bad habit of burying people first came into fashion. The carriage-panic at Bull Run, with the scared drivers lashing their horses into foam, may have been the same thing on a larger scale; but nothing in all former history could pretend to match it. Poor old Uncle Ben Robinson probably never rode so fast in his life, as he went to his grave!

For obvious reasons the curtain may be drawn over what followed. The hearse had been abandoned by the driver not far from the cemetery; but there were enough of us—the steady ones—*i. e.*, those who had not been to the wedding,—to keep watch over it until Domine Stanton and the flying crowd came back, with very white and sickly-looking countenances, and performed the last rites of burial.

My impression is that Major Jeff Taddlewick, who still lives to be the crying nuisance of the whole country around him, has never yet ceased bragging of his exploit. His *dirtiest* trick of a lifetime, and necessarily the one which best contented him, originated the Two-Forty Funeral. Everybody agreed, of course, that the wedding-breakfast at Captain Bob Hollis' made all the guests sick; but I am not sure that Captain Bob knows to this day, how the breakfast came to be so unhealthy. If not, I beg to take this method of informing him; and I only hope that he may yet take occasion to break every bone in the body of the perpetrator.

XVII.

SAM BROWN'S MUSH.

Boiled Indian meal, or corn meal, under its various names of "mush," "suppawn," "spawn," "hasty-pudding," etc., is, with milk, as popular a preparation as ever made an American Oliver Twist hold over his bowl a second or third time and ask for "more." It does not often excite the enthusiasm of the poet or the constructive skill of the romancer; but that it has the power to do the former in some instances, the good old poem of Joel Barlow bears witness; and that it can inspire a story which has nothing whatever to do with the imagination, let this brief sketch give evidence.

Mush, with *real* milk accompaniment, is so popular, that it may almost be called a "national dish,"—quite as near to it, at all events, as doughnuts and baked beans. It goes with a slippery lusciousness through the cherry lips of the New England girl, resting for an hour from her labor in the factory or the kitchen; it forms a very acceptable "pudding" to the coarse meal of the laborer on the farm or the railroad of the Middle States; it filters through the ivories of the Georgia negro on massa's plantation (always provided said negro has not suddenly become contraband, run away and left the house desolate). It is everywhere, where the quiet delights and comforts of the country are known; and there is at least some imitation of it in the restaurants of the city.

Sam Brown was very fond of mush, and had a pretty numerous family who were equally so. The time was some five-and-twenty years ago, when primitive food and fashions were much more in vogue than they are at present; and the section was very near the place of my own residence at that time, where homely comforts were plenty enough, but luxuries almost entirely unknown. Though Sam was no farmer, he had a "lot" and a few acres of pasture ground, which afforded sustenance more or less abundant to a couple of cows of any other breed rather than the short-horn Durham or the gentle Devon. The milk from these cows was, of course, the leading dependence in the way of food for the family; and though it was cooked and served up in nearly every way known to rude cookery, it was oftener fated to disappear down the hungry throats of Sam and his family, in company with enough "mush" or "suppawn," to elevate it to the condition of lively "spoon victuals," than in any other mode of preparation. In those days, in the section of country where Sam lived, and in families no more wealthy than his, it was customary to boil a pot of mush almost every day, have it smoking hot for supper, cold for breakfast the next morning, and perhaps a part of it sliced and fried as a substitute for hot bread at dinner.

I should say that Sam was a shoemaker, living in Bushy Hollow—a kind of "boss-journeyman" if such phrase may be coined for the occasion—himself and two or three apprentices doing the work for manufacturers living in the country towns adjacent, as the practice is still followed in some portions of the Eastern States. Space and fuel were both objects of no small consequence to persons in Sam's pecuniary circumstances; and the benches for himself and the boys, in winter, were consequently arranged along the wall of the kitchen, and the same fire that warmed them did the cooking for the family. The continual running in of Mrs. Polly Brown or some one of her four daughters from the sitting-room, to look after the welfare of the particular pot of food that happened to be over the fire, made an agreeable variety for their work; and Sam and his apprentices generally had a word and a joke with them nearly every time they made their appearance, considerably heightened in spice by frequent applications to the little black jug, which the "boss" kept under his seat, and passed round with commendable equality whenever he happened to fancy that he was thirsty.

One day the big iron pot was hanging over the fire in that room, with water set to boil, and to be thickened with corn meal for mush whenever it should reach the boiling point; and Sam and his apprentices were sitting as usual at their benches, hammering and stitching away, Sam with two or three drinks of whiskey under his waistcoat, and consequently a little jolly, and the boys exceedingly comfortable, to say the least of it. Artists in mush manufacture know that the water requires to boil just enough and not too much, before it can be "thickened" to advantage, and that the thickening must be done with a dainty hand, and the proper quantity of stirring for every thimbleful of meal that falls into the water, in order to prevent such a calamity as its being "lumpy."

On this particular occasion the fire was slow, and the big pot of water, awkwardly hung a foot from the fire on clumsy trammels, was very dilatory about getting up to that heat which would have made it of any use to Fulton. Mrs. Polly Brown had come in two or three times to inspect the progress of the pot boiling—found the prospect unsatisfactory, and gone out again. At last, well along in the afternoon, Mrs. Brown made another entry, took another look at the pot over the fire, saw that though it did not quite boil it was on the verge of a simmer, and so went to the cupboard, took out a sugar-box of salt, holding perhaps a couple of quarts, sifted in the necessary handful to salt the pot of mush, put back the box, and went back to her work.

Only a little while had elapsed when Sally, one of the daughters, came in and took a survey of the pot, altogether ignorant that her mother had lately been in the vicinity. She, too, found the water at a simmer, and not ready for thickening. So she, too, went to the cupboard and got the box of salt, and put in what she imagined to be the requisite quantity for seasoning. No one stopped her, though all the shoemakers saw the operation. One of the apprentices was about to do so, when a sharp "hist!" from Sam told him that there was fun in the wind, and kept the meddler silent. So Sally concluded her salting and went out, while Sam indulged in a quiet chuckle over the fact that the mush might be the least in the world *too* salt, if many of them played at cross purposes and each attended to it.

Fate seemed to favor the mischievous, if not the brave, on that occasion; for Kate, another of the daughters, happened to be crossing the room to go to the loft, only a few minutes afterward. As she passed, she happened to cast a glance at the pot—saw that it did not quite boil—thought that she could save coming in on purpose, by just salting the mixture while she happened to be in the room—went to the cupboard, got the box and salted it again! This time, as may be supposed, the apprentices understood that Sam intended to have the mush just as salt as the fates ordained, and made no attempt to interfere. Kate went on to the loft, with a consciousness of having done her duty; and Sam, when she had closed the door, fell back on his bench in a perfect convulsion of laughter—one of those half-suppressed chuckles that made him red in the face and threatened strangulation. He laughed for about five minutes, till he found relief in the tears that ran down his cheeks from the pain of a stitch in the side; and the apprentices joined him with a good will, though it is probable that they did not see all the fun of having their supper spoiled.

When Sam had finished his laugh, he took a mode of repairing the damage caused by the women's blunders, which certainly would not be adopted in Secessia during the present dearth of salt, in which they spank the babies and hold their heads over a barrel in order to catch the briny tears. His operations showed about an equal disregard for the value of the salt and the quality of the mush—ordinary tastes being consulted. In other words, he got up from the bench, went to the cupboard for the salt-box, opened it and poured the entire contents—perhaps a quart or thereabouts, into the pot—after which he sat down and resumed his work very demurely,

Not long after, Mrs. Polly Brown made her appearance again, found the water boiling merrily (it might have been, by that time, one of the boiling salt-springs so famous for invalids in certain localities,) and thickened it. Nothing was said by Sam or his apprentices, though the latter had some difficulty, it is probable, to keep from exploding over the nature of the mixture at which the housewife was working in such good faith. Once more replaced on the fire, the preparation boiled away cozily again, and by supper time it was to all appearance capital "mush."

In honor of the fun that had already taken place and the other fun that was coming, it is to be supposed that Sam passed round the jug that afternoon a little oftener than usual, for when he went to the supper table the twinkle in his eye was very droll indeed, and the apprentices had quite enough toddy in them to make them capable of enjoying any mischief that might turn up. When they came in to supper from a short "lark" they had been enjoying in the yard, the mush was smoking hot in a large dish in the centre, and bowls with milk were arranged round the sides of the table, with a big earthen cup of molasses for such as might prefer the preparation with that sauce. If Mrs. Polly Brown had been a very acute observer of the human countenance, she might have discovered, as she did not, that the large dish of mush was a mine, all ready to explode into mirth if it did not blow up her domestic tranquility.

Sam took the big pewter spoon that stood in the middle of the smoking preparation, ladled out a portion into his bowl, and helped each of the apprentices to a corresponding quantity. By this means all the males were provided before either of the females had an opportunity to test the cookery. Sam, with a droll twinkle in his eye, ladled a spoonful out of the milk in his bowl, put it into his mouth, and with several audible "tsits," proceeded to taste it. The effect on the inside of the mouth must have been very like that said to be produced on the outer cuticle by the sudden plunge of a thin-skinned man into the Dead Sea; but the apprentices followed suit, and audible "tsits" went round the table. Evidently something must be wrong, to judge by the expression of the male faces; but *what*, the female portion of the family had no idea.

"Why, Polly Brown!" Sam finally broke out, after rolling the compound around in his mouth until it had nearly pickled the tongue and palate—"why, Polly Brown, you havn't put a bit of salt in this mush!"

"Havn't I?" said Mrs. Polly. "Good gracious!" Then suddenly remembering the very act of doing so, she repelled the unhousewifely suggestion. "Yes, I did—I *know* I did! I remember salting it before the water boiled!"

"Why, mother!" spoke up Sally, "then the mush must have been salted twice, for I am sure that I went in and salted it, just before it was thickened! Don't you remember I did, Pa?"

"Did you ever!" said Kate, the second girl. "Why, there must be salt enough in it, then, for I am sure that *I* stopped when I was going up stairs, and salted it!"

"And I'll be cussed," said Sam, breaking away from the table, running to the cupboard, bringing out the empty box and throwing it upon the table, preparatory to rolling over on the floor in a convulsion of laughter that fairly shook the room—"I'll be cussed if *I* didn't salt it!"

There was a matrimonial storm, shortly afterwards, in Bushy Hollow, Mrs. Polly Brown loudly accusing Sam of having "spoiled" the mush, though how any one could have spoiled it after its having been three times salted, remains a question. For the truth of a story in addition, ever since told in the neighborhood, I cannot vouch, as I *can* for that already recorded. That supplementary story is to the effect that Sam's pigs were fed with the over-salted compound, it being found unavailable for household use; and that the effect of that quantity of salt on the animals was such as to *cure them in the pen*, so that when killed they proved to be salt pork and never needed pickling! But whether the pigs were salted or no, there is not the slightest doubt of the saline qualities of Sam Brown's Mush.

XVIII.

PAYING OFF A PARTNER.

It is no matter of any consequence on which one of the great newspaper streets of New-York the following incidents occurred—what was really the name of the newspaper in the office of which they took place—or how many years have elapsed since that period. It is enough to say that they did occur, under my own immediate observation, and so long ago that a good many of those who laughed most heartily at the time have probably forgotten all about them.

I was at that time sub-editor, proof-reader, writer of puffs and moral essays, and general man of all work for "a paper of wide circulation and extensive influence," which I may designate as the *Weekly Balloon*, from the simple fact that I might some day find my nose pulled if I gave the real name.

The *Balloon* was the joint property of two proprietors, who at the same time both officiated as responsible editors,—the one, Wilson, looking most after the business affairs, the reading of the longer manuscripts, and the column of "Answers to Correspondents;"—and the other, Burke, passing judgment upon the poetry and short sketches received, making selections, writing short stories, occasional but very rare indulgences in longer ones, and having the literary and belles-lettres charge of the paper generally. Both had been practical printers in early life, and entered the editorial profession through that legitimate channel.

No two men could be more dissimilar, either in person or character, than Wilson and Burke, though they agreed capitally—perhaps for that very reason. Wilson was a tall man, of gravely classic face, though with a merry twinkle in his blue eye, that showed how capable he was of appreciating a joke. He seemed the very pink and pattern of strict morality, and I have no doubt that Mrs. Wilson, a neat little round-faced woman, who used occasionally to drop in at the office of an afternoon, in time to have Wilson go home with her to tea—thought him so. The *fact* was, that he had an irresistable propensity for a pretty face, and a still more overpowering one for a neat ankle, and that oftener than semi-occasionally he fell into delicate flirtations with the lady-contributors who visited the office, the extent of which I never had any means of ascertaining. He was decidedly handsome, and that fact, perhaps, had spoiled him a little and given the small dash of feminine frolic to his character, to which I have alluded.

Burke was the very antipodes of Wilson. He was short and stout, with a head of curly black hair, and a face showing unmistakable marks of Hibernian blood, from which he was only a couple of generations removed. He was a jolly, rollicking, story telling fellow, fond of a joke, and with no propen sity to conceal the fact. Practical pranks were en tirely in his line, though he did not find occasion to indulge in them very often within the precincts of the *Balloon* office. I think he bore the reputation with Mrs. Burke, whom I also saw occasionally at the office, of being a regular little scamp among the women, while I do not believe that he ever went beyond a harmless jest with one of them. So much for his merry face and mischievous manner—two characteristics which often give men a dreadful reputation to which they are by no means entitled.

The editorial room of the *Balloon* was at that time arranged into three divisions. In the outer, which ran the whole length of the room, I had my desk, while two or three others for the mail-clerk and for chance contributors were distributed about the walls and partitions. The other half of the room was again subdivided, and in one of these halves Wilson had his desk, while Burke had his in the other. All the room was open at the top, so that voices could be heard when persons were in loud conversation; but no one could either see within the room of the other, or hear what was said in a tone of voice pitched at a low conversational key.

As I occupied the outer room, and was there almost all the time during business hours, I necessarily saw all who passed through into the rooms of either of the proprietors, and I sometimes acted as a sort of lazy usher—(keeping my seat all the while)—to direct unaccustomed visitors to the proper apartments. The *Balloon* had a large corps of lady-contributors, nearly all of whom brought their own manuscripts to the office and made the necessary arrangements for publication. Burke had the larger proportion of these visitors, while I noticed that on the average those who visited Wilson stayed much the longer.

I was scribbling away at my little desk one day, engaged in the melancholy occupation of writing up the "humorous department" of the paper, without a particle of humor either in myself or my material,

—when a lady came in at the office door and enquired for Mr. Wilson. I not only directed her to the door of his private den, but on that special occasion got up to show her across the room. The lady had a roll of manuscript in her hand, and in that respect looked like any of the five hundred lady visitors. But while the majority of them looked decidedly *passé*, (don't let the literary ladies suppose that I am slandering them!—literary talent, whether in man or woman, seldom ripens so as to be available, until the first roses of youth have died from the cheek)—while the majority of them looked decidedly *passé*, I say, this woman was really a Cleopatra of dark beauty. I remember her looks, and even her dress, (which was of light plaid silk, robe and mantle, and the mantle heavily quilled,) to this day. Heavy masses of curling black hair—magnificent dark eyes, with lashes that swept her cheek—a rose-bud mouth and cheeks of peachy bloom that had never been bought at the perfumer's—a figure of queenly height and proportion,—all these I caught at a glance; and if I had not been a poor devil of a sub-editor, without even a private room or a license to fall in love, I should have been thoroughly intoxicated with her in the short space of time that she required to cross from the outside door to that of Wilson's sanctum.

As it was, I only fell so much in love as to be able to describe her at this distance of time. She passed into Wilson's room, and very soon a low murmur of conversation sprung up in that quarter. Though I could not distinguish the words, I could easily recognize the difference between the two voices. Very soft and sweet was that of the lady, while Wilson's seemed low and tremulous, indicating that he was somehow "knocked off his perpendicular," as Burke occasionally used to say of him.

This probably lasted half an hour, and then I heard the moving of chairs, as if the visitor was getting up to take her departure. Directly the door opened, and Wilson came out with her, his face all aglow with pleasure and excitement, and hers, it seemed to me, scarcely as calm and equable as it had been when she went in. Just as they passed out and Wilson was about to show her the extraordinary courtesy (for *him*) of accompanying her across my room to the outer door, that of Burke's room opened, and he came out, with his pen in his mouth, ostensibly looking for his scissors, or the paste-pot, (there was no mucilage-pot ready at hand in those days,) or some other very important trifle.

I had an idea then, and I have never got over it, that Burke did not really want anything, but that he had heard the female voice for some time in his partner's room, knew when they were coming out, and had determined to see what manner of woman it was that could keep Wilson's attention so long. If that was his object, he accomplished it, for he caught a fair view of the lady as Wilson handed her out of the door, and I heard him give vent to an emphatic "phew!" as he recognized her beauty.

"Wilson, who the deuce have you got there?" he asked, as the latter was recrossing the room to his own door. "She is as pretty as a picture!" he added.

"Is she? well, I did not notice," was the reply of Wilson, though his voice and manner betrayed him, and he was evidently excited if not agitated.

"Humph, you old rat! I know better than *that!*" commented Burke. "Catch *you* letting a handsome face go without noticing it! But who is she?"

"*I* don't know," said Wilson. "I know that she bothered me a long time about a roll of manuscript that she brought with her, and that she made me promise to read it this week and say whether it will be used, in our 'Answers to Correspondents.' I promised her that to get clear of her."

"And you don't know her name?" again asked Burke.

"No," said Wilson, though I think that he was telling a very permissable fib. "I only know the name she left on the roll of manuscript, to be answered by."

"Well, what is that?" persisted Burke.

"You seem to take a good deal of interest in her," answered Wilson, "for a stranger. The name on the manuscript is 'Julie.'"

"Humph! sounds French," said Burke. "Pretty woman, any how you can fix it!" and he went into his own room, closed the door, and I suppose went to work. But I caught a glance of his eye as he went through the door—a glance directed out of the corner at Wilson, and I saw there was mischief in it, though I had no idea, as the Westerners say, where the lightning was going to strike.

For that day, in the details of my business, the occurrence passed out of my mind, and I do not remember that I thought of it again until two days after, when the proofs began to come down stairs for my reading. They came in a huge bundle, as usual, fifteen or twenty at once. Running down the galley that contained the "Answers to Correspondents," I struck directly upon the name of "Julie" and instantly recollected it as the same that had been given by the pretty woman. I find a copy of this notice in my scrap-book, made from recollection a few days after, under circumstances which will soon explain themselves. It reads precisely as follows:

"JULIE.—The MS. has been examined. The style of composition is admirable, and the story exhibits a highly cultivated taste which cannot fail to bring the writer into eventual celebrity. We have made arrangements for immediate publication."

This was altogether out of the common order of our notices, and especially different from Wilson's grave and business-like style of communicating with correspondents through the paper. I saw at a glance that my first idea had been correct—that Wilson had really been very much smitten with the lady of the dark eyes—and that he intended to make his court to her and probably induce her to make frequent visits to the office, by paying her this marked compliment—a kind of compliment, the delicious sweetness of which to *young* writers, *old* ones become almost too much hacknied to recognize. However, all that was no business of mine, and I only make this explanation of what I understood from the notice, because it has a bearing on what comes after.

There were no serious errors in the proof, that I remember, and if any there were, they were certainly corrected, for a revise was taken, and *that revise Wilson himself read*—a very fortunate circumstance for me, in connection with any further employment as proof-reader in that office, as it afterwards appeared.

It is not to be supposed that having once read the proof, and examined the revise, I should again have seen the matter before it went to press; nor was it at all likely that any other person would read it, either in type or on another proof, until it appeared in the paper. It is pretty evident that nobody *did* read it, except perhaps *one*. However that may have been, the week wore on and the

Balloon was published—all fair, smooth and satisfactory.

I was sitting again at my desk, the day after publication, when a rather loud-voiced and rough-faced man, of a decidedly foreign aspect, entered the office. Neither one of the partners were at the time in their rooms. The visitor angrily asked for Mr. Wilson, in English only a little broken, and I answered him, of course, that he was out. How soon would he be in? I did not know, Be in to-day? I supposed so—might not be gone for any length of time. Would the visitor wait? He said he would, and *did* wait, slamming himself down in a spare chair with force enough nearly to knock through the cane bottom, and slapping a big switch against his boot, with an air which indicated that he would like to have slapped something else with it. I wrote on, but uncomfortably, with an idea that I had a volcano behind me, which might blow out at any moment.

After half an hour of waiting, and when my new friend had apparently found himself a little cooled, I heard Wilson's deliberate step coming up the stairs, and he came into the room the moment after. As he did so, I turned to the man in the chair and said:

"There is Mr. Wilson—you wanted to see him."

The man in the chair sprang up as if a galvanic battery had been suddenly applied to him, rapidly crossed the room to Wilson, pulling a newspaper out of his pocket at the same time, opened the paper, slapped it with his switch, and burst out in language not enough broken to need reproducing it in that particular:

"Are you Mr. Wilson? What the d—l do you mean by abusing my wife?"

"Abusing your wife?—who is your wife?—I do

not know what you are talking about!" exclaimed Wilson, slightly starting back.

"Then look here!" said the loud man, slapping his hand on the paper this time, instead of the switch. "You call my wife 'depraved' and 'abominable!' My wife never was depraved or abominable!"

"Who the d—l *is* your wife!" broke out Wilson, now about as angry as his visitor.

"My wife has been writing for you under the name of 'Julie,'" said the loud man. "You promised to look over her story, and she said you were a gentleman. But I see you are a big blackguard!"

"Take care!" said Wilson, with a motion that looked ominously like an intention to strike, which he evidently reconsidered. "Your wife—Julie—I did not say so about any such woman! Where the d—l is what you mean?"

"Here!" thundered the loud man, handing the paper to Wilson with another slap of the hand. I saw that it was a copy of the last *Balloon*. Wilson took the paper—read—rubbed his eyes—read again—then burst out with one single word that told several volumes:

"D——nation!"

I have seldom seen a man so angry. He rushed to the desk where I was yet sitting—threw down the paper on it with a slam, and said:

"What the d—l does all this mean? Didn't you read that proof?—that proof—*there?*—'Answers to Correspondents'—'Julie'?"

"Of course I read it!" I said, "and so did you, for I saw you! What is the matter?"

"Yes, I *did* read it myself!" said Wilson, "but there was no such cursed stuff there *then!* See what it is, *now!*"

He gave me time, now, to read, and I read. The

notice, the original of which I have before given, read at that juncture as follows:

"JULIE—The MS. has been examined. The style of composition is abominable, and the story exhibits a highly depraved taste which cannot fail to bring the writer into eventual misery. We have made arrangements for immediate destruction."

Some printer had dextrously changed "admirable" to "abominable," "cultivated" to "depraved," "celebrity" to "misery," and "publication" to "destruction"—making, it will be observed, rather a marked difference in the tone of the notice!

Perhaps Wilson did not wish to have me for a witness to any more of the conversation, for he invited the loud man inside. I have no doubt he made any quantity of explanations, offered to publish the matter the next week, and tendered a thousand apologies to the aggrieved lady, *if she would only come after them.* I heard some of the words, especially those of the husband, though not enough to give me the chain of his observations. Whatever may have occurred, the loud man did not look in much better humor when he came out, and I noticed that he took the roll of manuscript away with him. It never came back to the *Balloon* office (I may as well say here) nor did the lady of the dark eyes ever again cross the threshold while I remained in that employment.

The visitor had scarcely gone, that day, when Wilson came out of his room again, came up to my desk, and said:

"Do you know any thing about this cursed trick? Yes or no, upon the word of a man!"

"Upon my honor I do not know anything about it," was the answer I made, and I do not believe that he really suspected me. The next moment I heard his long legs going up the stairs that led to the composing room—two steps at a time. For what happened there I had afterwards the word of the foreman, and it was only what might have been expected—a number of angry enquiries on the part of Wilson as to who had meddled with the matter on the galley—denials on the part of the printers that any of them had done so—the end of all which was that the mystery was not cleared up in the least degree, except that the printers were exonerated.

Wilson made a straight guess at the perpetrator of the prank, however, I fancy, from the first. I am very sure that *I* did, from the moment of reading the altered paragraph. Some night during the week, when all the printers had gone home, Burke had quietly gone up to the composing room—made the alterations, in the midst of diabolical chuckles over the scrape into which he was getting Wilson, and got away again, as the newspapers say of the pickets who burn buildings in the occupancy of the hostile army—"without being discovered." It was not Wilson to say a word to Burke on the subject, even if he had had proof of the operation. He naturally preferred to dissemble his chagrin and "pay him off" when the proper time should arrive.

That time arrived, not many months after, though long enough for Burke to have relaxed the strictness of his watch for a "lick back."

Burke was really a very spirited sketch-writer, and he wrote longer stories, when he would enter upon the labor, that won and deserved popularity. He won that success, too, when he did strive for it, without plunging at all into the deeply sensational or "blood-and-thunder" style of literature. For anything of the latter class he had a most unmitigated contempt, and would about as soon have taken a dose of strychnine as willingly allowed his name to be appended to anything of the school of romance which has furnished us the "Fiery Fiend of Fiddlefaddle" and the "Last of the Blood-Tubs."

Burke finally commenced a story of English life, one week, after gathering an immense amount of material for a tale which should run through fifteen or twenty numbers. What the name was is now a matter of no consequence. He had an unlimited number of characters involved, and managed them, in the opening chapters, with extraordinary skill. Sharp, keen character-sketching, with trenchant wit, graphic descriptions of scenery, criticisms on art and literature, and all the pleasanter and more refined characteristics of the novelette, were the staple of what Burke evidently designed to make his master-work, to which he of course put his full name. As many other story-writers do when editorially connected with the papers to which they are contributing,—Burke wrote his numbers from week to week as they were wanted, instead of finishing up the whole story before the commencement of publication.

The tale had been running for some seven or eight weeks, and the interest was just beginning to be fairly evolved, when Burke was suddenly called to go East, by some property business there. He went away, expecting to be back again in two or three days, but was detained much longer than he expected. Finally a letter came from him, saying that he had been very busy—that he could not yet be home for a day or two—that he could not furnish the number of the story for that week—and that it would be necessary to make an apology to the readers and promise it for the number following.

I handed the letter to Wilson, who was at the time in his room, and asked him what was to be done about it. He swore a little over the fact that all the influence of the story on the circulation of the paper was killed by the break, and wished every man who commenced publishing a story before he had done writing it, was in some unpleasant subterranean locality. Just then the foreman, who knew of Burke's absence and had not heard anything of the instalment of the story, came down stairs to look after it. This set Wilson into a renewed rage, which, however, broke directly into a chuckle for which I could not see any especial reason.

"Never mind," he said to the foreman. "Wait till to-morrow morning, and we will try to find something that will do to fill up the space." The foreman accordingly went up stairs again.

A few minutes after I saw Wilson come out into the outer room, and get the hanging-file of the current volume of the *Balloon*, which he took in with him. From that time I did not see anything of him during the entire afternoon, except once or twice when I had occasion to go into the room for a moment, in which instances he was scribbling away at his desk with railroad speed, paying no attention to anybody or anything. Towards night I saw him send up to the printers a large roll of matter, and supposed, of course, that he had been supplying the vacant space of Burke's story with some lucubrations of his own.

When the story-proofs came down to me, late the next day, I altered my opinion as to what Wilson had been doing. With a full recollection of the prank played by his partner in the "Notices to Correspondents," Wilson had not been supplying the place of Burke's story, but *supplying Burke's story itself*. And such a supply! Burke had intended the story to run at least two or three months longer, but it had no after occasion to run, or do anything else, after that—it was finished!

It is impossible to particularize, at this distance of time, and as I have no copy, the contents of that wonderful three or four columns. But I distinctly remember that he brought all the characters over to this country, took them to the West, introduced an Italian bandit, two or three Arabs and an elephant, and in the concluding chapter killed off no less than eleven of the prominent personages, by various cruelties, from duels and taking poison, to the blowing up of a powder-mill, and the running off a whole train of cars into the Mississippi! It was certainly a most stupendous performance; and there, at the head of that fearful mass of droll impossibility and absurdity, stood the name of Burke as author.

Exactly in that shape the conclusion of the story went out to the readers of the *Balloon*. If it did not quite satisfy the readers who had been interested in the original story, I fancy that it furnished as much amusement as could well have been extracted from the same space in any human language. The general impression was, I believe, that Burke must have written these concluding chapters while suffering under a severe fit of the delirium tremens, and that the stuff had crept into the paper without Wilson's seeing it! That is about as near, by the way, as human calculations generally come to the reality!

It was two days after the publication when Burke reached the city. Somebody had shown him the paper, and his condition of helpless rage may be imagined, but if it is to be described somebody else than myself must make the attempt! When he reached the office, Wilson was sitting in his room, writing, probably, and very quiet. Burke strode across the outer room, his face stormy as a thundercloud, flung open the door of Wilson's room, strode in, and broke out—

"Who the d—l and thunder——"

He did not get any further with the question at that moment, and I think he never did afterwards. I heard Wilson interrupt him, and I could fancy him lying coolly back in his chair as he did so:—

"——The same fellow, I suppose, who altered my answer to a correspondent, not long ago! Do you know who *that* was?"

Burke's reply was a laugh. He was conquered. They went out together a few minutes afterwards, and I have an idea that they might have been found moistening their clay somewhere in the neighborhood. At all events, they were both quite as good friends as usual afterwards, and no quarrel had grown, as I was afraid might be the case, out of "paying off a partner."

XIX.

HOW WATTY BRIGGS DIED, AND HOW SQUIRE HORTON RESURRECTED HIM.

It is not usual to consider death a subject for merriment, and yet I submit that there are circumstances in which the name of the grim old monster may be used in close juxtaposition to a broad laugh. If the readers of this sketch do not agree with me that the unfortunate demise of the hero was a very funny circumstance, and that his return to life was one of the drolleries that one may properly remember for a lifetime—I shall stand convicted of having trifled with a very serious subject, and pay the penalty of public reprobation.

Among the residents of the country village of Edgewood, where I happened to be located a dozen or more of years ago, was one Walter or Watty Briggs, a jovial, hearty, intelligent and well-to-do man, who blended the two incongruous occupations of house-builder and small farmer. The former had been the "trade" to which he was brought up; but when he had amassed sufficient property to become the owner of a small landed estate, the smell of the freshly-turned earth had produced the same effect upon him that it has done upon many a man before and since, and spoiled his steadiness in his former occupation.

Briggs, farmer of twenty or thirty acres, had at the time referred to almost ceased to be a house-builder. Unlike the majority of the changelings, he prospered fairly though moderately, and became the unembarrassed proprietor of a neat little residence, with well-stocked out-buildings, and all the conditions of comfortable living. His family at that time consisted of a wife and half-a-dozen children of ages ranging from three to thirteen; and he and they held a flattering place of respect in the community.

It was at this time that Watty Briggs fell seriously ill with erysipelas—a disease often lightly regarded, but one that has few more dangerous rivals when it has a tendency to mount to the brain. For two or three days Briggs was confined to the house, and several of the neighbors had called upon him; but no bad results had as yet threatened, and no one doubted that the disease would soon run its course and leave him fully restored.

It happened, however, that a day or two before succumbing to the disease, Briggs had made a bargain for a pair of horses, with a man residing at some distance, who was to deliver them at his residence on a certain day. That day came when he had been some days confined, and when he was really very ill. When the report was made to him that the new horses had made their appearance, the anxiety of the thrifty farmer triumphed over the prudence of the man, and he petitioned to be assisted to the window, so that he could see his purchase. This favor was accorded by Mrs. Briggs, and the day being a raw and cool one in November, the result was that a sufficient chill was brought on in a few minutes, to drive the disease to the head, and that with the imprudent exposure, and the excitement of mind connected with the horse-purchase,

Watty Briggs was a raving maniac an hour after, the erysipelas apparently settling on his brain, and his life really in danger.

All the people of each small country village are of course aware when any well-known resident is sick; and the day following every resident of Edgewood knew that Briggs had exposed himself, taken a sudden relapse, and was rapidly sinking. His death within a few hours did not seem improbable, and his family were nearly distracted. That afternoon, in common with many of the neighbors, I went to the house to see the sick friend from whom I might soon be called to part; but when I reached the house I found a state of affairs existing for which I was not in the least degree prepared.

Watty Briggs was dead!

That is, Watty Briggs *said* he was dead; and he certainly ought to have known more about his own physical state than any of his visitors, or even the doctor! And as a droll old sea-captain once remarked in my hearing, of a lady who screamed out, in the extremity of some temporary pain, that "she was dying!"—here was a man of unimpeachable veracity proclaiming that he was dead, and why should we not believe it?

He lay upon his back, covered up in the bed, neither incapable of speech or motion, and not half so much emaciated by sickness as I had expected to find him. His eyes were open, though staring a little like insanity, and his facial appearance was not improved by the white cloths that bound his head. I should not have taken him for a dead or even a dying man, but for his personal assurance; though it was not difficult to perceive that the disease was really preying upon the brain, and to know that such a hallucination would probably exhaust him in a few hours, so as to give disease and death the victory.

"How do you feel, Mr. Briggs?" I asked, going up to the bedside.

"Me?—I don't feel at all!" was the reply.

"Ah!" I said, "that is a little singular. Men generally *feel* quite as much when they are sick as when they are well."

"Humph! yes," said the invalid—"sick men, but not dead ones! *I* am dead."

"Indeed!" I said, "when did you die?"

"About two hours ago," he replied. "I have been dying all day, and about that time the old fellow got the best of me."

"Sure you're dead?" I asked.

"I should be a fool if I wasn't!" he replied, a little sulkily. "I know *something* yet, if I *am* dead! They are going to lay me out by and bye. Mrs. Briggs is making the shroud, now!" and then he tried to look round towards the head of the room, where his wife sat at the time, sewing on a shirt.

"When are they going to have the funeral?" I asked, satisfied that there was no use contesting the matter with the monomaniac, and anxious to see how far he would go in his hallucination. Mrs. Briggs evidently considered the question a cruel one, for she burst into tears and left the room, while some of the other visitors shook their heads at me and laid their fingers on their lips.

"Well, I don't know," said the dead man, "suppose they will bury me sometime this week, for I've no doubt they will be glad to get me under ground!"

Very soon after, Mrs. Briggs made her appearance with a basin of some description of gruel intended for the sick man. She came up to the side of the bed, raised his head on the pillows, and made preparations to feed him with a spoon.

"What is this stuff, Mary?" he asked.

"Gruel, Watty. Come, eat it, like a good fellow! It will make you well."

"I tell you I am dead, and I *can't* eat! Gruel for a corpse! Did you ever hear of such cursed nonsense in your life?" appealing to me.

"I never did!" I said, and felt that I was quite correct in the expression.

"There, take it away and don't bother!" said the dead man. "Get my shroud done as soon as you can, before I am so stiff that you can't get it on."

Thereupon Mrs. Briggs, who was a very good, tender hearted little woman, again burst into tears, and went away with her gruel, waiting the coming of the doctor.

"Lean down here," said the dead man, "I want to say something to you that all the rest must not hear." I leaned down. "Do you know what Mary is hurrying that shroud so for?"

"No, not exactly," I answered.

"Well, I'll tell you!" he said. "She wants to get me buried and out of the way, so that she can have a chance for Tom Kelsey!" From that moment, though the married life of Briggs and his wife had been uninterruptedly happy, apparently, I knew that he had been at some time really jealous of Tom Kelsey, a good-looking railroad-conductor on one of the lines in the neighborhood—for half-crazy men, like drunken ones, give expression, during their mad periods, to thoughts which they carefully conceal during their lucid hours. Fortunately Mrs. Briggs did not hear the remarks, nor has she probably ever known, up to this time, that her husband had any such suspicions of her regard for the railroad-conductor. Several other neighbors coming in, I left the dead man for the time, promising to call again in an hour or two, and taking a very comical order, meanwhile, to carry to the coffin-maker. Two hours after I called again, and found no change in the patient, who held his hallucination about as before. While sitting by his bed-side, this time, and hearing his not-over-reverent speculations as to what would become of him in his new state of existence, on account of his having refused to make his appearance among the "mourners" at a late meeting, which he seemed to think had most probably sealed his spiritual fate,—while we were thus engaged the Doctor's sulky drove up, and that important person entered.

The dead man seemed to survey the medical attendant with very cool speculation in his eyes, but did not speak to him.

"Don't you know him?" asked Mrs. Briggs, apprehensive that he might be so far gone that he had forgotten the physician's face.

"Know him? yes, that's the Doctor!" was Watty's reply.

"Are you not glad to see him?" was the second question, delighted to find that the brain was not wandering at all points. Could the answer to the question have been foreseen, I do not think it would have been asked, for here was instance of unpleasant candor No. 2.

"Glad to see him? No! He's a devil of a humbug! Gave me all kinds of nastiness until he killed me. Now, I suppose, it will take just all the property I leave to pay his bill!"

Judging by the redness of the doctor's face, I apprehend that he did not discover the joke of the reply, especially as he was *not* notorious for the proportion of cures he accomplished, and *was* a little notorious for the length and weight of his bills!

Probably he never had so well-directed a thrust during all his professional life. However, he made the necessary examinations of the patient, but as he could not be induced to swallow a mouthful of anything, seemed a little disconcerted and a good deal puzzled, though a man of unquestionable skill and faithfulness.

I seemed to be at the scene of action in the midst of arrivals; for a heavy wagon rolled up while the Doctor was yet sitting in the room, and an elder brother of the dead man, who resided at some distance and had been sent for when Watty's situation began to be considered dangerous,—came in with his wife and daughters.

"Here is Joseph, Watty," said Mrs. Briggs, bringing him up to the bedside, "Brother Joseph—don't you know him?"

"Know him?" said Watty Briggs, looking at him as contemptuously as if he had been speaking in our own times and asked to strike hands with Floyd or Wigfall—"Know him? I should think I did! He managed to pull the wool over the eyes of the old man and cheat me out of my share of the property! Yes, I know all about *him!*"

The deadly character of this shot, which constituted specimen of unpleasant candor No. 3, may be judged from the fact that the elder Briggs had died not many months before, the possessor of a handsome property, as everybody supposed, but a one-sided will leaving Joseph nearly all of it, and the other sons only a pittance each. Everyone believed that undue means had been used by the elder son to induce the formation of such a will, but probably not an unpleasant word had been spoken in reference to it by the younger, until that revelation of real feeling through the veil of madness. After that, however, I have an impression that Joseph Briggs always understood the private opinion borne of him by his brother, and that he feared him accordingly.

In this crisis of affairs I once more left the house, and did not return to it that evening. I heard from Briggs early in the morning—that he kept his hallucination unbroken, took no nourishment nor medicine, and was gradually sinking. The Doctor believed that he would die in a few hours from this action of the brain, unless some means could be found to break the charm; and neither he nor any of the friends seemed to have any power to get the monomaniac to sleep, or to persuade him that he was yet in living condition. Argument, entreaty, ridicule—all had been tried, and all to no effect, and the case was really growing hopeless.

At this interesting stage of the proceedings at Briggs', a new actor made his appearance on the scene.

Squire Horton, an influential resident of Edgewood, and a very intimate friend of Watty Briggs, had been absent from home for some days, and only returned on the night which followed the conversation I have recorded. He was a man of strong common-sense and much joviality of disposition, as had already have been demonstrated in many instances in the neighborhood. I saw him, early in the morning informed him of the precarious state in which Briggs was lying, and asked him if he knew enough of his friend's habit of mind to be able to trace out any plan for breaking the illusion which was killing the victim without any real aid from disease.

"Humph!" said the old Squire, after getting a full relation of Briggs' proceedings. "Humph! I don't know what can be done: *something* must be done—that is clear! Let us go up and see how he is getting along."

We accordingly went to the house, where, except that the patient was weaker, there had been no change since the preceding afternoon. Briggs still had his eyes open, knew every person who entered, and had the power of motion. He was just as "dead" as the day before, however. The doctor had almost given him over, his family had grown so hopeless that they did little else than furtively watch what they supposed to be the death bed, and cry in odd corners.

We entered the sick-room, Squire Horton ahead, and I watched very closely to see what he would do, aware that all would depend upon his striking the clue at once, if at all. The old Squire nodded to the family, said, "How-de-do, Briggs?" and then began to "Sniff! sniff! sniff!" as if scenting something terribly unpleasant.

"Why, what is the matter, Squire Horton?" said the dead man, who recognized him at once. "Smell anything?"

"Smell anything? I should think I did!" said the Squire, going to one of the windows and throwing it open. "Why Mrs. Briggs, how *can* you live in this room with the windows down?"

"*I* don't smell anything"—said the dead man—"I mean *they* don't smell anything—*I'm* dead!"

"Oh, I know that," said the Squire. "That is exactly what is the matter. You are dead, and you ought to have been buried before! You smell terribly!"

"*I* smell? *I? I?*" murmured the patient, who had not before seen the thing in that light, and evidently did not like it when he saw it.

"*You* smell? of course!" said the Squire, "Every dead body smells after so many hours, and you ought to have been in the coffin and under ground yesterday. Has the coffin come, Mrs. Briggs?"

But Mrs. Briggs did not hear. Entirely overcome by what she considered the last cruelty to her poor dying husband, the wife had fled the room, uncertain what to do, and once more in tears.

"Well, if the coffin has not come, we must see about it!" said the Squire. "We can't have men left rotten above ground in this way!" and he indulged in another "Sniff! sniff! sniff!"

"Squire Horton," said the dead man, changing his position decidedly, for the first time in forty-eight hours, and half-rising on his elbow—"Squire Horton, I don't believe one word you say! I *don't* smell, I know I don't!"

"Pooh! pooh!" said the Squire, "You're dead—what the deuce could you know about it! You stay here, M——, and see that they keep the windows up, while I go out and hurry one of the men after a coffin!" and out of doors went the Squire, as if fully intent on his errand.

Poor Briggs!—I looked at his face as the Squire went out, and saw that he was sadly troubled—that the chain had been struck, to some extent, even if not effectually. He could agree to be dead, and *insist* upon being dead, but the idea of smelling so that the windows required to be raised—paugh!

Squire Horton had gone out of the back door, and I went to the back window to watch him. I saw him standing by the watering-trough of the well, his face screwed into a very comical expression, and for a moment I did not know what he could be doing. Directly, however, I saw his motion, though I could not understand his purpose. It was, as I have said, late in November, and the watering-trough for the horses had been skimmed with ice all the morning. The water, of course, was at a fine Arctic temperature for bathing. Into the trough the Squire had thrust his right hand to the wrist, and was holding it there, letting it chill thoroughly, while the absorption of that quantity of cold was causing his face to make the queer grimaces I had noticed.

After standing there for perhaps five minutes, he turned and entered the house. Merely winking his eye to me, he went up to the bed where Briggs lay, and pretended to arrange the clothes. Instantly, however, I saw him dart his right hand under the clothes, inside of the bed, and in about half a second more I knew that it had effected a lodgement somewhere about the most sensitive parts of the dead man's body.

"Ough! ough! ough! o-o-ough!" yelled poor Briggs, as that lump of human ice touched his warm body, and as it fastened closer to him he writhed and yelled on, and finally sat bolt upright in bed, spite of his weakness. All the members of the family heard the yell, of course, and all ran in, expecting to find the poor man dying in convulsions.

"Well, what is the matter?" coolly said the Squire, withdrawing his hand, and looking as if *he* was the party outraged, if any one.

"Matter?—Squire Horton!—thunder!" gasped the dead man—"you are freezing me! Why your hand is like ice!"

"How do you know?" calmly asked the Squire.

"Know? why, I *feel* it!" said the monomaniac. "Ugh!" ugh!"

"Ha! ha! well, that *is* a good joke!" laughed the Squire. "You, a dead man, feel my hand! Come, now, that is too much! We can't believe that, you know! Lie down like a good fellow, and be dead, and wait till the coffin comes!"

"What does he say?" said the invalid, clapping both hands to his head, and seeming to be wrestling with some mighty thought. "Cold hand—couldn't feel it if I was dead—*did* feel it—why, I am *not* dead after all! No! Squire Horton, come and shake hands with me!—Mary, come and kiss me!—and some of you shut down that window. What a fool I have been! I am *not* dead, after all!"

The scene which followed may well be imagined. I have no intention of trying to describe it. Half an hour after, the tension removed from the brain, a little nourishment administered, and then a gentle opiate,—Watty Briggs lay sleeping quietly, and *saved*. A week afterwards he was walking over his grounds, his face baldly scarred with erysipelas, but a well man. That he was not before that time in his grave, and as rotten in reality as his droll friend had pretended, I believe was not in any degree owing to the efforts of the Doctor, but to the practical demonstrations of his vitality so oddly given by Squire Horton.

XX.

STARVATION BY RAILROAD.

My friend Brown travels occasionally, and semi occasionally. His carpet-bag may be seen (a small carpet-bag it is, and holds little more than a change of linen, a book or two and a tooth-brush)—at any time and in any place between the St. Lawrence and the Gulf of Mexico; and his traveling-cap is coated and re-coated with deposits of dust blown from every sand-hill and clay-bank between the Atlantic and the Rocky Mountains. Brown travels for the excitement of the thing, as well as from some occasional suspicions of business in one place and another, which just furnish him a sufficient excuse for what he calls "taking a short run," that "short run" ranging from a hundred miles to two or three thousand. Merry and a little waggish is Brown, as the conductors and brakemen on many roads, and the steamboat clerks on many rivers, can testify. If you look at the book he is reading in the cars, you will not often find anything more abstruse than "Verdant Green" or some one of Peterson's "Humorous Library;" and when he takes cold from the improper opening of a car window on the back of his neck, he holds that a hearty laugh will always shake the cobwebs from his throat. Brown is always just in advance of all the accidents—half a dozen steamboats having exploded and a dozen or two of railroad trains having come into collision or run off the track the day after he had passed over the line, and no catastrophe ever occurring to his own particular train or steamboat. Such is Brown —now for Jones.

My other friend Jones very seldom goes out of the city. He is a book-keeper in a down-town office, very devoted to his business, and with a snug penny laid by in unimpeachable stocks against that "rainy day" which he has always been expecting and which has never come. A trip to Boston by way of the Sound, and a run down once or twice in a summer to some of the sea-side watering-places, comprise pretty nearly all of his absences during a round dozen years. Fond of the good things of this life is Jones, and a free, not to say an inordinate eater. If he has a horror, it is of being deprived of his "three meals a day," besides occasional lunches which he dodges round the corner to get, or carries from home in the morning, wrapped up in a piece of white paper, under the guardian care of Mrs. Jones.

A few months ago, before travel between this city and Washington began to have the charm of danger and consequent excitement—before Baltimore hoisted a secession flag or General Butler was heard of outside of Massachusetts, Jones having suffered for a month with nervous head-ache, induced by too close attendance to his columns of figures,—Jones contemplated taking two or three days' recreation. At this time his evil fortune favored him with a call from Brown, who had been uncommonly quiet in the city for a week. Jones mentioned his intended exodus, but was doubtful whither he should go. Brown considered for a moment, and then suggested that he (Brown) was going to Wash ington two days after, and enquired whether Jones had ever seen the "National Bear Garden?" Jones had never seen the "National Bear Garden." Why should not Jones go to Washington with him, by way of Philadelphia, unless he (Jones) had been frightened off by the then current exposure of the terrible dangers haunting the passage of Big and Little Gunpowder Creeks, &c., (not consequent upon the bridges being burned—that was an after event;—but upon their supposed likelihood to tumble down from instability.) Jones had *not* been frightened by any such exposure, and had his doubts whether the whole statement was not a humbug. He knew Smith, who had been over the road within a week, and who said that the people did *not* creep fearfully out on the platforms while crossing, and that the trains were *not* in the habit of tumbling off into the river. Would Jones go, then? Jones still hesitated. Why? Subsequent enquiry on the part of Brown established the fact that Jones was anxious on account of his diet. He had heard that the opportunities for dining on these routes were very bad—going without food for too long a time made him dyspeptic and gave him the headache still worse, and ——. Brown stopped him short by the assurance that if he would go, he (Brown,) being an old traveler, would take care that he (Jones) should not suffer in that particular. So urged, Jones consented to trust himself to the tender mercies of the railroads.

Brown and Jones were to go by way of the Camden and Amboy, leaving at six o'clock in the morning, an hour inducing chilliness and objections to an empty stomach. Coming down by the cars to the Astor House from their separate boarding places in Bleecker and Houston, and walking thence down to the Battery—Brown, who had resolved religiously to keep his promise to Jones, and on no account permit him to starve,—Brown suggested to Jones that although he, (Brown) through the kindness of his landlady, who had risen very early, had had an early breakfast consisting of a round of toast, half a dozen eggs, and a cup of coffee—he (Jones) had probably had no breakfast? None, Jones answered. Brown thereupon suggested that Jones had better patronize one of the *al fresco* coffee-and-cake saloons in the neighborhood, while he, Brown, would smoke a matutinal cigar. Brown took the hint and invested in a cup of strong coffee thereat, three hard boiled eggs, a modicum of corned beef, and two plates of greasy butter-cakes.

Half an hour after starting, the breakfast-bell rang on board the Belknap—very much, apparently, to Brown's surprise, who declared to Jones that he never before heard of such a thing as their having breakfast on board the Camden and Amboy boats. However, if Jones would go along, he did not care if he himself went down to the breakfast table and "took a bite." It was well, he gravely remarked, to eat whenever one had a chance, in railroad traveling, as half the time nothing could be got, below. Jones assented, and they went down. There Brown trifled with an omelette and a roll, and imbibed a couple of cups of very good coffee, while he succeeded in loading Jones with six inches square of tough steak, a few fried eggs, some slices of cold tongue, rolls, a leg of fried chicken, coffee, etc. Jones expressed himself as "full," while Brown remarked that he wouldn't be, before he reached Philadelphia. Half way between Amboy and Bordentown, Brown purchased a dozen oranges and a large paper of burnt almonds, half of which he managed to make Jones consume, while he smuggled the remainder into his own carpet-bag, to be given away to the first family of obstreporous children he might happen to meet.

By the time they reached Philadelphia the ride had so much consolidated Jones' food, that he was easily persuaded to believe himself hungry, especially under Brown's occasional reminder of the lack of eatables on the southern end of the route. A blending of boiled fish, roast beef, and half of one of the plum pies for which Bloodgood's is so famous, was dexterously engineered under Jones' waistcoat by Brown, who took care that his plate should be persistently supplied with tit-bits during the whole half hour of sitting. Jones looked a little plethoric and showed incipient symptoms of asphyxia, as they took the carriage for the Baltimore depot; but these passed away in half an hour. Fifteen minutes were allowed at Wilmington for "refreshments," and these Brown improved to remind Jones that it would be late when they reached Washington, and that at the crossing of the Susquehanna there was always such a crowd as to make obtaining a mouthful a matter of difficulty, besides the probability that the Marvellous Woman of the Susquehanna might snap off the head of any unlucky passenger who chanced to ask for food without tendering payment in advance. He was rewarded by seeing Jones bolt a sandwich, two hard-boiled eggs and three doughnuts, and liquify them with a tumbler of milk. At Havre de Grace the crowd was *not* so great as Brown had anticipated, and the friends *did* succeed in securing a place at the table while the boat was crossing, in spite of the old woman's attempts to prevent their finding anything to eat. Brown felt it necessary, here, to eat ravenously, and did so without much difficulty, having fared lightly during the day. Under this incitement Jones came up manfully, being assured by Brown that this was the last chance before reaching Washington—and two luke-warm oyster stews, a side of chicken, a few slices of bread, and pies, with coffee, went down before his determined attack.

This last feather had broken the camel's back. Jones fell back upon his seat in a state of partial stupefaction, as the train rolled away from Havre de Grace—his eyes protruding, his face surcharged with blood, and serious symptoms of apoplexy. Not even the change of cars at Baltimore could arouse him to eating one of the half dozen oranges which Brown then and there bought and pressed upon him. Jones declined supper at his hotel that night, and two days of danger of brain-fever on his part, with a doctor's bill to pay and two days of nursing on the part of Brown, made up the sequel of the affair. It is not believed that Jones will hereafter, travel he where and when he may, take any extraordinary precaution against *railroad starvation*, or that Brown, if they again travel in company, will again take the same amount of pains to stuff Jones into asphyxia.

Meanwhile my very good friend, and the most popular of travelling-managers, Captain Simpson, who commands the Camden and Amboy railroad boat, must be careful how he supplies too plentiful breakfasts and thereby add to the temptations of the travelling Joneses.

XXI.

TWO BIG SHOTS AT WILD-FOWL.

THERE were, in the time of my sojourn in the classic neighborhood of Bushy Hollow, twenty years ago, any quantity of sporting characters, thereabout, and almost every man kept his gun in his house, ready loaded for game. Every mechanic, too, kept a loaded gun in his shop, ready for a chance shot at wild fowl, bird, squirrel or rabbit. Let me record two of the most effectual shots made —one by each of two residents of the section.

Of the two parties, both were very respectable men, and both past middle age, but with enough of the glow of youth still in them to make them fond of a good joke and able to chuckle very good-humoredly over it when fully accomplished. One was a hatter, grave and precise in his personal appearance, thin and lank as Shakspeare's "ribbed sea-sand," and the last man in the world whom one who did not know him would ever have suspected of a "sell." The other was a laboring man, short, chunky, and jolly in face and figure, as droll outside as the first was grave, and fully keeping up the character internally.

I had observed, one day, that Tom Robbins, a rather good-for-nothing neighbor of mine, had been manufacturing a lot of decoy ducks, or "stools," as they were called, which the uninitiated only will need to be told are exact imitations in shape and size of the various kinds of wild ducks, painted in a rough resemblance to the bird, and capable of deceiving a flock at a distance into the belief that one of their own kind is on the ground or the water, as the case may be. I had seen Robbins on a scaffold adjoining his house, painting the "stools" aforesaid, and in the afternoon he put them on the edge of the flat roof of his house to dry in the sun.

Early in the morning—in fact before it was fairly light, Burns, the laboring man, happened to be coming up the street, just by Bird, the hatter's, and very near Robbins'. Bird was just coming out of his door as Burns came by, and they stopped to say good morning.

Suddenly Bird looked up towards Robbins', and made an espial. "Why, look!" he said to Burns, in a half-whisper, "only look! If there has not settled a whole covey of ducks on the eaves of Tom Robbins' house!"

"So there has!" said Burns, without a thought that ducks were not supposed to be in the habit of alighting on the roofs of houses—"So there has! By gracious, what a shot, though, if I only had my gun!"

"Take mine," said Bird, very kindly, "she stands just behind the door, and by good luck loaded with duck shot. I have plenty of poultry, and don't need them. Take her and bang away."

"You are very kind," said Burns, "I will." And he stepped in, took the old king's-piece and let fly into the thick of them. Not a wing was raised; not a duck stirred. "What in thunder can it mean?" said Burns, "that not one of them stirs!"

"Mean?" said Bird, with a roguish twinkle of the eye, "why you have killed every one of them so dead that they have not had *time* to stir. An excellent shot, Burns, certainly."

"Y-a-a-a-s," said Burns, who somehow began to think that there was something a little out of order in the affair. But at that moment, Robbins, who had been a bed in an upper chamber very near the eaves of his house, opened the door in a wondrous hurry, and about half scared to death. He saw that Burns had a gun, and burst out with—

"Why, was that you, Burns? What the Old Harry do you mean by shooting at a man's house in this manner? The shot came rattling against the side of my chamber rather too thick for comfort, and one of them broke my window. What have you been shooting at?"

"Ducks," said Bird; but Burns didn't say anything.

"Ducks where?" said Robbins, with a look at the top of his house.

"Why, up there on the eaves," said Bird, still managing to keep the laugh back. "He seems to have killed the entire flock."

"Ducks, thunder!" said Robbins, between a laugh and an oath. "Them's my stool ducks, put out to dry. You have done it!"

"Possible?" said Bird.

"Possible!" said Burns; "yes, and you knew it, you old humbug! Never mind; I'll pay you for it, some day."

Burns paid, if I remember correctly, some three dollars for the damage done by his shot, while Bird went off home, his long lean frame shaken by a convulsive chuckle, and his thin, sober face screwed up to the nearest similitude to a laugh of which it was capable. After the adventure, Burns did not show himself for a week. When he did, he took a public roasting that was worse to bear than the expense of paying for Tom Robbins' stool-ducks.

Two or three years passed away, and Burns had never had any opportunity for repaying Bird for his trick. They were excellent friends, and Burns took the occasional quizzing which Bird gave him on the subject, with the air of one who should say, "Well, you are too smart for me, and I give it up." But he had not forgotten it, and the opportunity for payment came.

One day Burns happened to pass the head of "Wilson's Pond," a saw-mill pond in the neighborhood, within a quarter of a mile of the village; and he observed that Wilson had brought home with him from a trip to the southward, two very fine specimens of the tamed wild goose—a valuable aid for the goose-hunter, obtained by breaking the wing of a young goose from a flock, and after healing up his hurt, clipping just so much of the end of the wing as to prevent his flying away. After a year of training, they will learn to perform their part to perfection, and seem to take delight in decoying others of their wild brethren down within reach of the gun of the hunter; though the fact is, no doubt, that they are merely calling for company, in their native language.

Wilson had procured these, and put them into his pond, as the fall was coming on, to nest there, and be ready for decoying any flocks that might pass, within reach of his gun, which had a bad habit of being stuck out from a loop-hole in his saw-mill.

Burns knew all this at a glance, and a very wicked but quite as natural desire to take revenge on Bird for the duck business, took possession of him. He knew that it would not do to attempt selling Bird himself, as the fact of the latter's trick upon him would make him suspicious of any suggestions in regard to wild fowl, in which he should appear. So he commissioned little Pete Dickson, a half-foolish and half-cunning fellow, who did half the errands of the town, with a promise of a dozen big apples, to run in a great hurry and half out of breath, and inform Mr. Bird that a lot of geese had just lit in Wilson's mill-pond.

Pete did his errand properly, and Bird took the bait, while Burns ensconced himself snugly in the mill, and looked out of the loop-hole.

Bird was very fond of wild fowl, and he seized his gun in a hurry and sloped for the scene of action. He hurried through the woods until he came very near the pond, when he began skulking after the manner of the most approved of deer stalkers or goose hunters; his long thin form half bent, dodging behind trees so as to approach the prey without disturbing it. Pete was close behind him with finger in mouth, and snickering under his breath.

At length, through the trees, he had a view of them. There they were, prime old fellows, and one of them "honking" most beautifully. Bird took a few steps, so as to bring them both in range—they seemed entirely undisturbed—and then he "blazed away." A better shot is seldom made; one of the pair "keeled over" at once, and the other, with wings broken and several shot in the body, tried to dive, and then lay helpless on the water.

Bird looked around for the punt, (a small boat) to get them, and as he did so, Burns *accidentally* came up the walk through the woods towards him.

"Why, what the Old Scratch have you been doing, Bird?" he said, as he saw the havoc, "Is it possible that you have been shooting Wilson's stool-geese?"

"Stool-geese!" gasped Bird, "you don't mean to

say that they're Wilson's. Why that cuss!"—and he pointed to Pete, who, half on a grin and half scared to death, stood with his finger in his mouth, behind him—"that cuss came running and told me there were some wild geese just lit in the pond."

"Y-a-a-s! well," said Burns, "he did not know any better, I s'pose. Poor Pete, you know, hain't got them all. But you've done it beautifully. This is worse than shooting wooden ducks!"

"John Burns!" said Bird, turning around and lifting his gun by the muzzle as if to strike with the butt, "you sent that snickering fool, I know you did. I've a great mind to brain you, as I ever had to kill a rabbit."

"Don't do it," said Burns, dodging, though without much idea that Bird would strike. "You don't think I would do such a thing! If they had been wooden ones, now, the case might have been different; but I couldn't think of having you hurt real ones, you know!"

Bird looked round at him again, and had another propensity to strike with the gun, but he didn't. He put the gun on his shoulder without another word to his persecutor, and struck a bee-line for Wilson's house, about a quarter of a mile distant, walked into the wagon-house where he was at work, pulled out ten dollars and paid him, and left without any explanation. Wilson did not know what it meant, but he discovered a little while after, when he went to the mill-pond.

Bird did not feel very friendly towards Burns for a few weeks, but the laugh was on him, and he found it the best policy to take it easily, especially as he had played the first trick. So he smoothed it over, and squared the account for the amount to which Burns had out-tricked him, by cheating him abominably in his hats for ten years afterwards, as Burns avers to this day. But neither of them, to the best of my knowledge and belief, though they may occasionally have tried duck and goose-hunting on more certain grounds,—ever took another shot at wild-fowl without having fair assurance whether it was *wooden* or a too costly description of the real article.

XXII.

DEACON JONES' MINCE-PIES.

Brown and I were strolling down one of the avenues one night, a little late, when one of the most remarkable coincidences occurred that I ever remember to have seen noticed. Brown, in the midst of a highly interesting conversation, (to me, at least), stopped suddenly, clapped his hand to that part of his waistcoat under which the stomach is supposed to be located, and uttered the single exclamation: I am hungry!" I made a rapid examination of ny own feelings, and in an instant, without clapping my hand on the waistcoat at all, was enabled to reply: "So am I!" This was the coincidence.

I found, directly after, that the feeling had probably been induced in both of us, from the sudden flashing of a couple of large restaurant-lights across the pavement. The light was no doubt electrical. Barker, who kept the restaurant, was and is notorious for the quality of his mince-pies. Mince-pies are the most scandalously unhealthy food known to humanity, especially for eating late at night. Therefore, Brown and I went into Barker's fully resolved upon eating mince-pies. Barker was behind the counter himself, and never were seen such pies as those he lugged out from their retirement for our special edification. Crisp, flaky-looking crust, with here and there a moist-looking spot through which the unctuous richness had oozed in baking, then partially dried and left a deposit as rich as that alluvial one supposed to be periodically left by the Nile when it ebbs away. Within, and between the crusts, a dark-brown mass of finely-chopped meat and pulpy apples, with here and there a raisin swollen almost to bursting, and little specks of pungent black currants. Below, the crust thin and flaky, but sodden with rich juice; and all the pastry part of the manufacture the nearest possible imitation of those astonishing *pates de foie gras* for which the truffles were furnished by demon hands, the dough rolled out by a witch with her broomstick, and in the purchase of which wonderful edible the Count de Perigord, of the old legend, disposed of whatever small amount of soul he had about him.

But the flavor—ah! there was the charm! Imagine all the subtle aromas and essences of all the delicious edibles of a century, concentrated so that they could be enclosed in an ordinary pie-pan, and there we had them. Imagine all the foams and sparkles that have ever bubbled on the brims of beakers, since Hebe held up the goblet of nectar for Jupiter—imagine them all, their exquisite fruity flavors compressed to a few drops, and all employed in adding delicious pungency to a mouthful!

Humph! what is all this? I have been growing maudlinly eloquent over Barker's mince-pies, and not a gratuitous mince-pie have I had from Barker to make up for the outlay of mentality and conscience! The long and short of it is, that Brown and myself ate three pieces of pie each, and that one of us certainly, and both of us probably, dreamed that night of having eaten a cord of stone-fence, or having one foot planted in our stomachs of those four elephants who, according to one of the oriental theologies, support the whole world on their broad backs. But the pie had an effect before this. Brown smoked a black Manilla cheroot after this late lunch, and sat very near the stove meanwhile. The result was that when he got up to leave the restaurant, he was as tipsy as he should have been after two bottles; while I, who had not joined in the segar, merely felt as if a hive of bees had been swarming in my head.

"Why, confound that cheroot!" said Brown, when we had reached the street and the cool air revived him a little. "There must be opium in that tobacco. If I did not know better, I should say that I was drunk."

"And so you are—and so am I, a little!" I said.

"Why, you didn't smoke at all?" suggested Brown.

"No, but I ate three pieces of Barker's mince-pie," I replied, "and if you knew as much about that mixture as I do, you would know that each is about equal to a bumper of brandy or two glasses of old port!"

"Pshaw!" said Brown, "do *you* repeat that old nonsensical idea that any one can get drunk on mince-pies? In the first place, there is very little liquor put into them; in the next place, what little they contain is evaporated in cooking; and in the third place—"

"In the third place, they act on the head very much as if there was plenty of liquor in them after all!" I interrupted. "Now, Brown, keep still, and walk as straight as you can, while I tell you a story about mince-pies."

The story I told Brown is the one which follows—the dramatis personæ being persons well known and still living, and the incident an actual one which occurred within the circle of my own acquaintance, and not many miles from the great city.

Deacon Jones was a very good sort of man. He had a fine house, elegantly located on the bank of one of the prettiest rivers in America; kept good horses; gave excellent dinners; had a bevy of handsome girls, as plump as partridges and as gay as larks; was exceedingly hospitable, and welcomed every visitor as if he had no other business in the world than to keep a caravanseria arranged for the accommodation of traveling people. Especially to ministers who might happen to be in the neighborhood, was Deacon Jones' a haven of refuge; and nowhere in the world could they find a more plentiful table, or sleep in softer beds, or find better attendance than there.

Mrs. Deacon Jones is not to be passed over, in remarks about the character of the Deacon. Deacon Jones was no more perfect without her, than Mrs. Deacon Jones without him, or one half a pair of scissors without the other. Deacon Jones was rubicund and jolly; Mrs. Deacon Jones was ditto. Deacon Jones was very fond of good living; Mrs. Deacon Jones was as fond of helping to eat the good things she made, as she was of making them. Deacon Jones was very susceptible to the name of being hospitable; Mrs. Deacon Jones was equally susceptible; and so on to the end of the chapter.

A few years ago—a few years ago was a period of time so like the present, that no perceptible change has taken place within that time in any member of the Jones family. The Deacon has perhaps a few more streaks of gray among his well-trimmed whiskers, and perhaps Mrs. Deacon Jones has one or two more showy bows on her dress cap, and some of the Misses Jones are married, and some more of them going to be. But there is no change worth noting in the family.

Well, a few years ago the Reverend Hezekiah Smith was about to spend a few days in the neighborhood of Deacon Jones', and contemplated making his home there for the time. Great preparations in the way of roast meats, doughnuts, mince-pies, etc., were made by Mrs. Deacon Jones and her pretty daughters, with the assistance of Nancy, the servant girl; so that when the reverend gentleman arrived, everything was in "apple-pie order," to use a favorite expression in the neighborhood, for the reception of the Domine and any friends who might happen to call in to see him during his stay. Mrs. Deacon Jones had never been more succcessful in her baking. Her pies were like a Seville orange, "rich, agreeable and juicy." Her doughnuts were puffed up to the degree that there was great danger of their bursting, and her roast meats were such as might have tempted a greater anchorite than Friar Tuck to forget the vow of abstinence over his parched peas.

Deacon Jones' family and "fixins" were all ready, and the Reverend Hezekiah Smith duly arrived. There was the usual quantity of warm welcome, the usual number of hand-shakings, and the requisite quantity of kisses bestowed upon the cheeks of the aforesaid Misses Jones. All was as cozy and comfortable as possible, and the Deacon was as happy as could well be imagined. The time wore on, and the Deacon and the Reverend Hezekiah were summoned from their comfortable place at the fire, to dinner. And such a dinner as it was! A superb turkey at one end of the table, a noble baron of beef at the other, bread of snowy whiteness, butter that only Mrs. Deacon Jones could make. And then the pies.

Such mince-pies as those of Mrs. Deacon Jones, are not to be found every day by those who do not know on what avenue Barker's is located; and the way in which the Reverend Hezekiah disposed of three large pieces, was only to be paralleled by the manner in which Deacon Jones himself disposed of five, and Mrs. Deacon Jones and the Misses Jones respectively of two or three apiece; everybody smacking their lips over the last particle, and declaring that *such* flavor, *such* spicy juiciness, never had been known before. To be sure, they were a little strong, but that was no doubt partly the effect of the exceedingly hard cider, which was always employed as an ingredient in that section, and partially of the liberal allowance of allspice, cinnamon and nutmeg, with which the good lady had flavored them.

Soon the gentlemen retired to the parlor, and the ladies busied themselves about the clearing of the table and other household duties. The Reverend Hezekiah and Deacon Jones took seats by the stove, and putting their feet as near the mantel as possible, began to discuss affairs generally. To the surprise of the Domine, the Deacon began to talk thick in a few minutes, and in a few minutes more he did not talk, he merely gabbled, and his eyes had a rather queer appearance. In a little while longer he let his head fall unsteadily over against the table, and was fast asleep, with a snore that would not have disgraced any bar-room in the banner ward of corner groceries.

"Well, I never!" said the Reverend Hezekiah, to himself. "Certainly, I never! If I did not know the character of Deacon Jones so well, I would make affidavit the man was drunk! Deacon! I say, Deacon, wake up here! Deacon, what's—hic—what's the matter?—hic—bless my soul, I never felt so queer in all my life! Heigho!" and he yawned. "I feel as if I really wanted to go to sleep myself. But I am—hic—really alarmed for the Deacon. Mrs. Jones!" and he got up and went very unsteadily to the door and opened it.

Stretched out on a chair, with mouth open, and in a very disturbed and uneasy slumber, was Mrs. Deacon Jones, with her face as red as a peony, and every indication of a genteel virago who had been on a spree. On a bench in the corner, was a juvenile Miss Jones, making a very sad attempt to comb her hair with a clothes-peg, while the rest of the family had disappeared.

"Bless my soul—hic!" said the Domine, "this is most extraordinary. What does it mean? I should say the whole family were drunk—hic—and I too, if I did not know better. Heigho! I may as well go to sleep, too. Bless my soul, what does it mean?" And the Reverend Hezekiah returned to his chair and went to sleep, as cozily as the rest.

About three hours after, a neighbor coming in on business, found the whole family asleep and awoke them. Such headaches as were current, were entirely unaccountable, as well as the sudden imitation of drunken slumber which had fallen upon the whole family,—until a comparison of notes revealed the fatal circumstance.

Mrs. Deacon Jones, after mixing her mince-pie material, had left the jug standing beside it, uncorked, and gone out. Young Master Jones coming in, had smelt the contents of the jug, found it brandy, liked brandy in mince-pies, and poured in a pint or so. Mr. Jones, happening to want the jug, to take to the neighboring village and replenish for medical purposes, had thrown what brandy there was in it into the compound, supposing that none had been put in,—washed the jug and gone off with it. The consequence was, that *about a quart of brandy had probably been consumed by the family in one dinner!*

Neither the Reverend Hezekiah Smith nor Mrs. Deacon Jones, nor yet the Deacon, ever liked, during the balance of my acquaintance with them, to be reminded of that particular visit, nor of that particular batch of mince-pies. It was said that the brandy jug was afterwards kept as carefully from the Master Joneses, as if it had been a bottle of corrosive sublimate or strychnine. And no wonder, when it came so near to making a respectable Deacon of the church a drunkard for at least three hours, and put a Domine in corresponding peril!

Brown was nearly sober by the time I had finished my relation; but he has since expressed his intention of prosecuting Barker for selling liquor without license, having become a convert to the faith that—whether lager-bier will intoxicate or not, mince-pies, properly charged with good old brandy, will make the clouds around the brain quite as rosy as if the fluid was imbibed from a tumbler.

XXIII.

SURROGATE COOKE'S URGENT REASON.

GEORGIA law has long been a proverb, and Jersey law sometimes comes but little behind it in the way of originality—not to say efficacy. I have some doubts, however, whether all the peculiar strings necessary to secure the rapid administration of justice in the latter State, are quite understood. In that belief I shall unravel at least one of the secrets, by the knowledge of which some one else may profit at no distant day.

In Jersey, as in most—perhaps all, the States of the Union—letters of administration on the estates and effects of persons who have died intestate, are issued by the County Surrogates. There, at least, whatever may be the rule elsewhere, a certain number of days after the death are allowed to elapse, in favor of the next of kin, before any one else can take out such letters. Failing any application on their part (which does not *often* fail) after that lapse of time more distant relatives, or those who hold no relationship to the deceased, if they can give proper security, are allowed to secure the letters.

When the deceased is supposed to have left a considerable amount of property, the securing of these letters is no small object, as the administrator always charges, and is allowed by the Orphans' Court (which body has tne final settlement of the estate) a pretty stiff per centage upon all moneys or representatives of moneys which have passed through his hands in the settlement.

Of course there are plenty of pettifoggers in all the country villages, who snuff the carcase of a wealthy intestate afar off, and who do not let the grass grow under their feet, when the legal delay has expired, before they make application on their own behalf for the "fat job."

Well—all this by way of preface. Not many months ago, Aunt Katie, wealthy spinster, who had been living in the family of Jim Doran—suddenly shuffled off this mortal coil—leaving, to every one's surprise and the grief of half a dozen—no will. Twenty-four hours after the death served to establish the fact; and Doran intended, as one of the next of kin, to make the requisite application the moment decency would permit. Less than three days—one beyond the funeral—would not very well answer for this purpose.

At the end of three days Doran made his application: letters of administration on the estate of Katie Doran, spinster, deceased, had been granted thirty-six hours before to Joe Shaffer, pettifogger and general business agent for the whole country—fast, in more senses than one. Doran was indignant, and pointed out the law, or at least the *custom*, which gave the preference to the next of kin.

Cooke, the Surrogate, was very curt about the matter—said he was very sorry to have disappointed Doran, but *there were urgent reasons* why he could not do otherwise than grant the letters to Shaffer. Doran inquired those "urgent reasons;" Cooke refused to give them. Doran was impudent, Cooke insolent, and the former left with the idea that the papers had been granted to Shaffer for the especial purpose of keeping them out of his (Doran's) hands.

Naturally indignant, Doran told the fact in every bar-room and at every public meeting. In a week, the story had grown in its proportions, to a statement that Cooke had refused Doran letters, from a knowledge of his general dishonesty. This was the feather that broke the camel's back with Doran, and he at once entered a caveat against the settlement of the estates by Shaffer.

This brought legal proceedings, a few days later, in open court, at a time when my usual luck of falling in with ridiculous phases of humanity led to my being present. Half the sporting men in the county seemed also to be present, for some cause or other which I could not at first understand; and a general raft of friends and relatives of the deceased spinster were also on hand. No other person than Doran interposing between Shaffer and his letters, the question lay entirely between the two. Cooke, the Surrogate, was obliged, under order of the Judge, to come on the stand as a witness to the regularity or irregularity of the letters. He did not come willingly.

"There were urgent reasons, Mr. Surrogate, the court understands," said the Judge, "why the letters of administration were granted to Mr. Shaffer, and were not to Mr. Doran, the next of kin?"

"There were," answered Cooke.

"You will be good enough to give the court those reasons," said the Judge.

"Can't do it!" said Cooke, after reflecting a moment.

"We insist," said Doran's counsel.

"The reason *must* be given," said the Judge, gravely.

"Perhaps we may get at the fact by degrees. Had you or had you not any reason to doubt the capacity of Mr. Doran, the first claimant?"

"None in the world!" answered Cooke.

"His honesty!" urged the Judge.

"No!" answered Cooke.

"The legitimacy of his connection with the deceased?"

"Oh no, not at all!" spoke Cooke, rather impatiently.

"Then what *were* the reasons?" asked the Judge, with dignity.

"Can't give them!" said Cooke, sententiously, but looking worried, and shifting his feet about as if he would much rather have been somewhere else than in the witness-box.

"Mr. Surrogate," said the Judge, very gravely, "the court will be under the disagreeable necessity of supposing, if this silence is persisted in, that some undue influence was brought to bear upon you by Mr. Shaffer, to induce you to grant him the letters."

This was too much for Cooke. "Undue influence" meant a "bribe," and Cooke knew it: to let such an imputation rest upon him was fatal, especially against his chances of election next term.

"The court wants the urgent reasons," he finally blurted out, "and the court shall have 'em, though it *is* betraying confidence. I had an Empire colt that could just go in 2:32 to harness, and I wanted the half of four figures, ($500) for him. Nobody came up to my mark till Joe Shaffer, and he *did*, the day before he got the letters. The Surrogate of this county isn't bribed, but he hasn't quite lost all feeling for the man that knows Empire stock and is willing to go the right figure for it!"

I am afraid that court was not the most dignified body in the world for the next five minutes. Doran got his letters, and Shaffer lost them. But everybody understands, since, the right string to pull with Cooke, when after letters of administration in a hurry!

XXIV.

THE SWINDLE ON POSTMASTER FOWLER.

Several years ago, when Ike Fowler was Postmaster of this city, gay, blythe and debonnair, boarding at the New York Hotel, with no prevision in his mind of the day when he would be compelled suddenly to evacuate his comfortable quarters and leave his fashionable acquaintances, for a doubtful life in Cuba and Mexico,—at that time, I say, when Ike was everybody's friend and favorite, he had yet some enemies who sought to deplete his purse, and through him beggar the government whose accredited (too long accredited) agent he was.

As the government was regarded as a swindle, and every one connected with it an accessory, various were the attempts made to swindle Mr. Postmaster Fowler, by different classes of society, under the laudable expressed intention of "getting some of the swindled money back again"—such as offering bad bills and bad pennies, making a letter slightly overweight, writing on the corners of newspapers, using stamps that had failed to be properly cancelled, etc., etc., etc. All this, of course, was to be taken without the slightest suspicion that the keen individuals performed those little operations for the sake of the profit accruing therefrom: they would have scorned such an idea! They were merely doing a stern duty in the way of showing enmity to the purse of Ike Fowler, and through him to the post-office department and the government.

Mr. Postmaster Fowler was badly victimized one day, during the summer of 185–, in manner and form following. It is to be understood that *all* these attempts to do the Postmaster and his employees did not (as they *do* not) succeed; but this was considered a "splendid success," in the language at about that time adopted for plays that paid their expenses, and books that did not fall still-born from the press,—and had it occurred a little later, after the other charming nomenclature was adopted, would have been denominated a "big thing" not "on Snyder" but "on Fowler."

Young Abrahams, son of Abraham Abrahams, of the firm of Moses, Abrahams & Co., of Chatham street, was the operator; and it is his giant swindle upon Ike Fowler, at that time applauded and duly set down, that is now to be given to the world. Young Abrahams had been brought up to consider "trade" an institution, and a new wrinkle in that line as something that must eventually entitle the lucky discoverer to a cenotaph—said cenotaph to be built in the form of an immense and almost endless succession of hats, placed one on top of the other, with the simple legend crowning the whole—"sheap!"

Young Abrahams was observed by my friend Tom Short, and everybody's friend Tom Short, one of the best-looking black-whiskered fellows in town, with a roguish eye and a propensity for a practical joke that made him one of the most popular fellows in existence,—young Abrahams was observed by Tom, one afternoon in the summer of that particular year, wandering in a peculiar state of inquiry, in the neighborhood of that dismal old cavern honored with the name of "the Post Office," and especially devoted to that use from the fact that it is, of all the buildings in town, the very worst that could possibly be selected for such a purpose. Young Abrahams' mouth was open, as if he was trying to see with that useful organ, his nose was turned up as if a shower was soon expected and his brains needed irrigation, and the hat thrown back on his head had a suspicious gloss, indicating that it had just been taken down from one of the shelves for that particular occasion, and a card removed therefrom with the mystical symbol "4s.," imprinted upon it. Young Abrahams was evidently new to the neighborhood of Nassau and Liberty, and was looking up at the cupola for the letter-box.

Tom Short was a benevolent man (he is so still, for he kindly accepted an office from Old Abe the other day, and then, only a few days after, favored the old gentleman still more by accepting the lieutenancy of a company in the —th and going off to fight the secessionists)—and he at once went to the relief of young Abrahams. That interesting youth, when enquired of, informed Short that he had a California letter in hand, and that he had been for the first time temporarily released from the shop-walking and button-holing business in Chatham street, to perform the responsible duty of mailing. Short advised him, as a friend, to procure fifty cents worth of stamps and paste upon the missive, hinting that that preparatory movement was necessary before putting it into the hole which he would show him.

Young Abrahams was thunderstruck.

"Vot!" he said; "pay monish for putting dish letter in a hole? Mein Gott, dat ish a sheat!"

Short suggested that whatever the swindle might be, the easiest way was the best way; and young Abrahams was finally induced to accompany him to the stamp-window, and invest fifty cents in stamps of various colors and values, to pay for which he overhauled all his pockets and brought out various dimes and half-dimes in different states of drilled holes, sweating and battery.

Subsequently my friend Tom continued his career of benevolence, by leading the juvenile but very promising Hebrew to "fresh fields and pastures new" in the shape of the California drop-box, where he happened to have a deposit to make himself. Abrahams came slyly up to the box behind him, and began a sharp investigation of the windows. He crouched down and looked through one dingy pane of glass; he raised on tip-toe and examined another; he flattened his aquiline nose against the gla·s and surveyed things inside generally. Short scented a different kind of joke from the one he had bargained for, and yet was a little puzzled. What could be coming? All that Hebraic acuteness could not possibly be wasted—something brilliant was about to be done.

At length after a thorough exploration of the glass and the cobwebs, young Abrahams approached his mouth very near to Tom Short's ear, and asked the momentous question, in a very sharp whisper: "Ish Mishter Postmashter Fowler here? I wantsh to know."

"No," answered Short; "he is not here just now."

"Sure, now—no varesh dat he can see me?"

"Oh, yes, sure! Why do you ask? What do you want of him?"

"Vy, look-a-here! Don't you say noshing and I'll tell you. Mishter Postmashter Fowler is tam schmart, but he find dat I am tam sight schmarter. Dey make me pay fifty centsh for dese little papers to put dish letter in de box. I pay it, and den I putsch de schtamps in my pocket, and drop him in de box mitout 'em. Oh, dey ish very smart, but I tam sight schmarter!"

So saying, and while Mr. Short was surreptitiously whistling, and apparently engaged in a speculation on the probable blowing off of the weathercock on the top of the building, young Abrahams slyly slipped the letter into the box, and having thus done Mr. Postmaster Fowler out of the California postage, took his way back to Chatham street, with the consciousness of having performed a good action, and a certainty that he had added at least one more hat to the pile in future to commemorate the colossal fortunes of the house of Abrahams.

Tom Short, like a good fellow as he was, in spite of the danger to Ike Fowler's digestion of knowing how badly he had been defrauded, immediately pitched into the Post-Office and put the whole force on their guard against a repetition of so immense a swindle, by telling it; and at the present writing I dare the possible vengeance of young Abrahams, of Chatham street, as well as recall Tom Short to the recollection of many friends, by repeating it at this time when all the laughter that can well be accumulated is desirable.

XXV.

FUN AMONG THE BOOT-BLACKS.

It is the New-York boot-black—him of the juvenile years, but the mature wit—him of the chunky figure and the trousers made over from those of his father or his big brother—him of the Hibernian descent, the round, jolly face, and a strong propensity for nick-naming himself and others, and investing in amphitheatre tickets at the New Bowery—of whom these brief and jolly reminiscences are to be recorded. He may be called "Shorty," or "Boots," or "Patsey," or "Winker," or "Sojer Bill," or "Mealy Pertaters"—in either case he is one of the family, and bears an unmistakeable family likeness. His stamping ground is the City Hall Park, and he has outposts at every hotel door, and at every three-cornered bit of ground below Union Square. Where his home is, nobody knows, any better than where the wild geese go to in summer, or what becomes of the dead donkeys.

When the old Brick Church on Beekman street and Park Row was standing, and especially during the last year of the existence of that institution, the sidewalk in front of the door and opposite that of the Park Bank, was the down-town head-quarters of the gang. The man who inadvisedly came into that locality with a pair of uncleaned boots, was required to run such a gauntlet of the boys, with their eternal cries of "black your boots, sir!" "shine 'em up!" and "do it in a minute, sir," that he was very mean, or very determined, if he escaped without surrendering to some of the jolly little privateers.

My place of business happened to be so located as to lead me past the Brick Church often several times a-day; and I formed quite an admiration for the persistent little fellows, and grew so well acquainted with them as to know many of their familiar sobriquets.

I happened to be passing, one afternoon in September of that year, in company with Captain Wash Ralling, then of the One Hundred and Eighteenth Ward police, whom everybody would recognize, under his real name, as a jolly good fellow and pleasantly fond of his little practical joke, and at the same time one of the most efficient detectives, and one of the ablest police Captains in the Metropolis. Probably not one in ten of the street-boys about town but knew him; and strict as he had always been in the performance of his duty, not one of the boys but liked his genial face, and could be encouraged into almost any description of mischief by his winning smile.

The boys were in full force as we passed the corner of the church, and none of them seemed to be employed, though it was just before three o'clock and there were a good many passengers going by continually. Captain Wash stopped, nearly opposite the door, and in a moment half a dozen of the boot-blacks gathered around him, looking up in his face as if they felt that *something* must be in the wind.

"Nothing to do, eh, Shorty?" said Wash, addressing one of the largest of the boys.

"Nuffin at all, Cap'n," said the boy, adding, with

a mischievous dive towards Wash's pedals, "black your boots?"

"No, not just now!" drawled Wash. "But why don't you stop some of these fellows coming by, and black their boots?"

"'Cause they won't," said Shorty.

"Yes, but *make* them!" answered Wash.

"Eh—eh! we *can't!*" said Shorty and the half dozen others in a breath.

"Oh, you don't stick to 'em!" said Wash. "Get fast—hold on to 'em—don't let 'em go till you've fetched 'em. Two or three of you try one man, if you can't stop 'em without!"

The idea seemed to amuse the boys, but they did not seem quite to realize that it could be put in operation. The smutty faces laughed, however. Just then a well-dressed man came by, going down towards Nassau street, and Wash nodded his head to Shorty and towards the passenger, with orders to "try him."

Shorty hesitated an instant, took one more look in Wash's face, and the moment after he was blocking the way of the passenger, down on his knees and brush in hand, with "black your boots, sir?"

"No, get away, I don't want my boots blacked!" was the reply, the waylaid man trying to pass on. But by that time Shorty had caught another nod from Wash, and grabbed his victim by the leg. He made another attempt to shake off his tormentor, with the only result of aiding him to get his foot perforce on the top of his box. At this juncture Coffee Joe, another of the gang, was ordered by the Captain to seize the other leg and hold it fast, and he did so. After one or two more kicks the victim stood still and Shorty blacked away at leisure.

It is astonishing how soon a crowd can be raised in New York, and how readily any practical joke can be put into operation in the same locality. Two or three persons stopped to see the man have his boots blacked perforce. In less time than it takes to relate it they were seized upon, at Wash's nod and suggestion, by others of the boot-blacking fraternity, in ones and twos. One after the other some of them caught the joke and submitted. Others stopped to see the sport and were caught in like manner; other boot-blacks saw that something unusual must be going on, and ran over from the Park; more feet were compulsorily lifted; more spectators gathered, and the work went on merrily.

In less than five minutes from the time when Shorty seized upon the leg of the first victim, more than twenty pairs of boots were being blacked on the single sidewalk bordering the Brick Church, between Park Row and Nassau street; a crowd of at least a hundred and fifty or two hundred persons had gathered on the street on each side, under the impression that some kind of accident must have happened. Shorty and his coadjutors were raking in (though they probably did not get paid for *all*) more sixpences than they had ever received in the same length of time since they commenced business; and Captain Wash Ralling was lying back against the railings and laughing himself red in the face at the success of his prank.

Captain Wash might have kept on laughing for the next quarter of an hour, and the crowd increasing all the time, but for the coming up of an acquaintance who knew the practical joker, at once divined that *he* must be at the bottom of the mischief, and soberly inquired "how much per-centage the boys paid him for supplying them with business?"

At that hint that there were two sides to the joke, Captain Wash moved on, the boys lost their sudden run of custom, and the crowd dispersed quite as rapidly as it had gathered. But there is not one of those boys, yet remaining in the business, who does not remember "the time when Captain Wash set 'em to work down by the Old Brick."

II.

My residence, months after, and when the Brick Church had fallen, was on the west side of Broadway, while my place of business was, as before, on the east. Walking down town I consequently crossed the City Hall Park every morning; and as the blocking up of the sidewalk in the erection of the brown-stone building, had driven all the boys from their old stamping-ground opposite the Park Bank, there was a double proportion of them along the walks of the Park, and more of a gauntlet to run than ever.

Some of the faces in that gang of boot-blacks were worth study, and attracted me amazingly—there was so much good humor in many of them, and so much high health and exuberant spirits amid the dirt and squalor. One face that I remember had merry mischief enough in it to have made the fortune of the owner under favorable circumstances. The Irish blue eyes laughed so merrily, and the brown, round little cheeks and dimpled mouth spoke so plainly of some rustic Hebe who had been his mother, that I could not avoid taking a fancy to the merry wretch in the patched corduroys. I remember thinking, at that time, what a pity it was that some wealthy person did not rescue him from his squalor, educate him, and give him a chance in the world—and what havoc among the hearts of the girls, in that event, he would make before he reached twenty. I have since thought that with his talent for mirth and mimicry, he ought to have been educated for the stage, as he would have made the very beau-ideal of that rollicking, roguish, devil-may-care Irish "boy," with his impossible hat, his little twig of shillelegh, and his song of "The Limerick Races," or "Molly Asthore," that Barney Williams plays better than any other man of the generation.

I accosted him one morning, and learned that his name was Mickey Callahan—that his mother lived in Elm street, and did washing—that he had a sister who was older than himself, and (as he said) a good deal handsomer, and that when he got old enough he was going apprentice to a mason, and expected to build whole rows of brick houses every day or two.

Mickey, after our morning's conversation, used to monopolize waylaying me, to small purpose. Scarcely a day passed, for months, on which I crossed the Park without seeing him. He would manage to dodge up at my particular crossing, as I entered, and always accost me, respectfully enough, but mischievously, while the other boys soon learned that he had some kind of a quasi claim upon me, and kept from interference. The claim did not amount to much, pecuniarily, for I wore cheap patent-leathers, and only had occasion to employ Mickey once in a week or two when they wanted sweet-oil. Sometimes for weeks I would not patronize him at all, but the failure would not prevent his running along a little ahead of me, every morning, looking up mischievously in my face, and calling out "black your boots?—shine 'em up?" simply because he knew that I did not want them blacked at all.

Finally Mickey called me to account one morning. "Sure yez oughtn't to be wearing thim patent-leathers, Captain! Yez don't be givin' poor Mickey a job at all! Och, why don't yez wear leather boots?"

"Do you *really* want to black a pair of leather boots for me, Mickey?" I asked.

"To be sure I do!" said Mickey, incredulous that such a question could possibly be asked.

"And you are sure that you'll black them if I give you a chance, for sixpence a time?" I asked again.

"Wouldn't I though? Shine 'em up! Yez could see your face in 'em!" said Mickey, his blue eyes flashing confidently.

"Well," I said, "I shall begin wearing leather boots in a few days, for winter, and then you can have a chance."

I think Mickey watched my feet still closer after that, as if he had acquired a new right to me. Certain it is that he "boned" me every morning, though I still adhered to the patent-leathers, and invited me to undergo a periodical polishing that he knew I did not want (on the feet, at least.)

One morning, however, when it had rained cats and dogs the day previous, and promised to repeat the operation before night, Mickey's sun rose, though the natural sun remained hidden. Stowed away in a dark closet of all household refuse, I had a pair of old grained-leather knee-boots, bearing date from the "hard winter" of two or three years before, when Broadway was knee-deep with snow and mud, all winter on the average. These boots, covered with dirt and mould, were exhumed from their burial, and at an expenditure of twenty-five cents I succeeded in getting Bridget to melt a cupfull of tallow and beeswax, and "grave" them (as the boatmen would say) thoroughly from toe to strap. When the operation was done, they weighed about two pounds more than before, and had an outer coat of the villainous grease, of the thickness of sheet iron, that no power could remove until it wore off, and that could be safely calculated to defy the elements for a month at least.

Thus accoutred and with trousers tucked inside my boot-legs, I trudged down-town, the labor being no slight one, I must confess, and the muddy sidewalks adding occasional splashes to the coating of wax and tallow, that made the boots anything but ornamental. I was slightly afraid that from the threatening weather and the mud, I might chance to miss Mickey. But no fear of that, in reality. Mickey was at his post, (the gate-post at the corner of Broadway and Chambers street,) and he recognized me, happily without remarking my boots.

"Black your boots, sir?" cried the little fellow, with his old mischievous leer.

"Yes, Mickey," said I, stopping, "this time you *may*. I have got on my leather boots. You have been a good boy, Mickey, and I have never let you black my boots before. Now you can black them before, and *behind*, and then you can have your sixpence."

Mickey had thrown himself on one knee and got his blacking and brushes ready, before he caught a view of the boots. When he did see them, I think I never saw so many varied expressions on any human countenance in the same length of time. A complete thunderstroke of astonishment that any man *could* wear such a pair of boots—a calculation how many boxes of blacking and how many hours of rubbing would be necessary before that abominable mixture could be rubbed off—the fact that they *never* could be made to shine, under any circumstances—all these, with a flash of perception of the ludicrousness of the whole affair, could be read in the jolly little face of Mickey Callahan, as I looked down at him.

Mickey was stumped! I had him!

"Well Mickey," I said, "why don't you go to work? Your sixpence is ready. I am in a hurry."

By this time two or three other boys had sauntered up, and seeing the position of affairs, began tittering, and one of them told Mickey to "shine 'em up!" This was too much. Mickey got up from his kneeling position. I did not know how he was going to get out of it.

Did I have Mickey, as I had supposed? Not exactly! After one moment's hesitation, the little fellow quietly held out his box and brushes to me, as much as to say: "There, you can black them yourself if you want them blacked *very* much!" or "You can take my hat!"

I had the impression, as I stumbled across the Park in my thick boots, leaving the boys laughing behind me, that I had not made any extraordinary investment in Mickey after all, and that I had carried about ten pounds of grained-leather down town for nothing!

III.

Only one other scene, in which the juvenile knights of the brush and box have a share, though fifty more instances instead of one might be given of their peculiar quality. This was a remarkable illustration of competition in trade, and of the effects of that competition when brought down to a small transaction.

I was sauntering across the Park from the Beekman street entrance to the City Hall, one day within the last year, when I came upon a knot of half a-dozen of the little irrepressibles, with trade apparently very dull, their boxes and brushes piled up against a post under one of the iron chains, and they individually and collectively engaged in some kind of a game of marbles which has always been too abstruse for my comprehension.

Just ahead of me another individual had entered upon that municipal territory, and was passing up the same walk on which the boys were carrying on the game of abstruse dexterity. He was evidently a Yankee, though not born in any of the Eastern States—a Jersey one, probably, come over from Communipaw or Hardscrabble, and his errand in town was written on his whole outward appearance. He was tall and lanky, and walked with the grace of a step-ladder set to locomotion. He had a narrow face, with sandy scrubbing-brush hair, with mean nose and diminutive eyes, (I had a fair opportunity to note all these particulars very soon afterwards,) and I would have wagered my two-dollars' worth of best hat that if he had a nick-name in the part of the country he inhabited, it was "Skimp," "Skin-flint," or something of the same complimentary character. In apparel he was gorgeously arrayed in a new suit of black with the creases of the shop-shelves yet apparent in it, having evidently been procuring a new outfit at one of the cheap emporiums of Chatham street. Gorgeously arrayed, all but his hat, which was a greasy felt broad-brim, —and his boots, which were stout calf-skin, unblacked, and red with the dust of his native plains.

These boots attracted the notice of the marble-players at once. Up sprang the whole half dozen, leaving the game to be decided afterwards, and made a dash at the adventurous foreigner with the new clothes. "Black your boots!" "Shine 'em up!" "Do it in a minute!" "Give 'em a nice shine!" and innumerable other incentives to invest sixpence in polish, were showered upon him from all the circle, while two stood in his way so that he could not go on without running over them, and the rest were all ready to seize him from behind at the least encouragement. I leaned on the iron chain not far off, pretended to be studying the flag over the *Tribune* office, and noted the adventures of Jersey.

"Black your boots?"

"No, get out of the way—don't want 'em blacked!" was the surly response.

"Oh, he oughter! See what nice clothes he has got on, and only look at them boots!" said one of the boys to the others, with an air as if *he* was not interested, but was merely making a philosophical remark for the general good of society. This flattery of the clothes brought the customer to a stop, as the incipient young diplomatist who had not yet emerged from the crysalis of boot-blacking, no doubt thought that it would!

"See here—dern it! no, guess I don't want 'em blacked!" said Communipaw, stopping short, nevertheless, and looking down at once on his new trousers and his red boots.

"Yes yer do! Shine 'em up!" answered the flattering person who had before spoken.

"Well, dern it, how much do you charge?" asked the customer, hesitatingly. "He who hesitates is lost," not less in negotiating with a body of boot-blacks than in direct intercourse with the Prince of Darkness.

"Oh, only sixpence!" said the boy who seemed to have acquired the right of preëmption, dropping at once on his knee and grasping his brush.

"Sixpence! oh, get out!" replied Skimp. "No, I can get 'em blacked home for less than that!" and he made a motion to pass on, as he had no doubt done two or three times that day while buying his clothes at the Jew shops in Chatham street.

"Do it for five cents," said the boy who had put himself in position, spitting in his now-opened box of blacking.

"No, that's a derned sight too much!" said Skimp, making another move to pass on. "Never give so much as that in my life, jest for puttin' a little blackin' on my *boots!*" (Emphasis on the last word, as if it might have been reasonable enough to pay such an unheard-of price for blacking something else.)

"Won't you give five cents? Eh, ain't you smart, now?" indignantly said No. 1, throwing his brush into his box, and jumping up.

"See here, fellers! Ain't none of you goin' to do it less than that ere?" queried Communipaw, who seemed now to have got in the notion of having his boots blacked if it did not cost *too* much. Business was probably very dull, for thereupon ensued a competition which is rare among the guild. (Your boot-black does not generally "cut under" his rival.)

"Yes, here, hold up yer foot! I'll do it for four cents!" said one of the other boys, unslinging his box and throwing himself into position.

"No, that's too much, too!" said the prudent person. "Tell you what I'll do—give you three cents."

"No yer don't!" broke out Nos. 1 and 2 in chorus; but No. 3, who was evidently hard-up and had a sort of a seedy, rat appearance, "went back" on the fraternity.

"I'll do it for three cents!" said that individual, throwing himself into the requisite position and dragging one of the feet on the box.

"Well now, black 'em nice, all over," adjured the foreigner, as the brush began to lay the blacking on the red leather, "Derned if I ever have 'em blacked again ef you *don't* do 'em nice!"

The juvenile of moderate charges worked away, making innumerable applications to the box of blacking before he could get that extensive territory of red leather covered at all; while the malcontents—that is, all the others who had "struck" from such a depreciation in the value of their labor—formed a corps of observation at the nearest post.

"Ony jest look at him!" indignantly cried different members of the gang. "Blackin' boots for three cents!" "Ain't you a smarty?" "Eeeagh!" "Want another box of blacking afore he's *half* done!" "Eeeagh! Eeeagh!" and this running fire of comment kept on during the whole operation, which was by no means a short one, for the country boots had evidently been made where leather was plenty, and the liberal customer pointed out two or three places where he wanted "a little more on," and "gin 'em another rub!"

Finally the work was done, the juvenile workman got up from his kneeling position, and the time for payment came. Communipaw's right hand had been jingling something in his pocket during all the process, and now the hand came out with a variety of contents which he put into the other. There was a knife, as I could see from my position—some cord—a comb—a few buttons. The dexter hand moved round among the assortment, but did not seem to find what it was looking for.

"Derned if I didn't think I had. three cents!" was the surprised exclamation. "Swan I had a little while ago. Wouldn't hev had 'em blacked ef I'd a knowed I hadn't 'em. Look a here, boy, here's one cent—that's all I've got, 'pears—give you t'other two next time I see you." And he dropped the single copper into the hand of the knight of the brush!

Here my knowledge of the circumstances and my descriptive power both fail. Which was driven and hooted out of the Park more particularly—the rat-boot-black or the man who got his half-acre of red leather blacked for a cent,—I do not know. I only know they all went down the walk towards Broadway, pretty rapidly and with a good deal of noise. I do not believe that Skimp has ever crossed the Park since, and I am not too sure that the offending member was not expelled from the privileges of the fraternity.

XXIV.

BILL FRASER'S BIG LUXURY.

THE best stutterer I have ever known, with the exception of Joe Bramby, elsewhere named in these recollections, was Bill Fraser, a legitimate descendant of the old Scotch Frasers of Lovat, and a brother to the Princess Lucien Murat, who kept a school at Bordentown, New Jersey, and now sustains the style of the Imperial Court at the Elysée Bourbon at Paris.

Fraser was a hotel-keeper, a horse-jockey, gambler and unmitigated scamp, known over the whole section of country stretching between the cities of New-York and Philadelphia—half the time tipsy and always stuttering, but so droll and jocular that plenty of men who despised him and his courses, still tolerated his company. He was always, in his palmier days, surrounded by a knot of wild fellows who helped him drink his liquor and spend his money; and a gay time they generally managed to make of it. Fifty anecdotes of his jocular scoundrelisms might be given, but we must be content with one which shows that there is a bound even to the extravagancies of the spendthrift.

There was a "protracted meeting" going on in a country church, not far from one of the villages where Fraser and his friends were carousing at the tavern. A "protracted meeting," as the uninitiated may need to be told, is a revival meeting, generally under the auspices of the Methodist denomination, but sometimes held by others, at which preaching, exhortation and prayer are kept up at short intervals, sometimes for many weeks, with personal appeals to those who may happen to be attendance, often not easy to resist, and resulting very generally in large accessions to the churches engaged.

To this meeting Fraser and his companions went over from the tavern, all half tipsy, and altogether reckless. Not much was known of them in that particular section, especially by the good people of the church, and consequently none of those engaged had the least idea what a valuable addition had been made to the audience with the entrance of the party. They took their seats quietly enough, in one of the pews not very near the pulpit, and the exercises of the evening went on.

The meeting had been held for several days, and was now in full progress. Preaching and prayer were mingled with exhortation and singing, and there was some noise and a good deal of excitement. At length some of the more fervent fathers of the church came down from the pulpit and the circle of prayer near it, and began to move about from pew to pew, making urgent personal appeals to all who showed the least signs of attention.

Some evil genius sent one of the good old deacons to the pew where Bill Fraser was seated, with half a dozen of his boon companions near him. Perhaps Bill was a little sleepy after so much whiskey—at all events he had his head bent down to the back of the pew in front of him, and the old deacon at once seized upon him as one whose head must be bowed by sincere contrition, and who must, consequently, be a hopeful subject! He bent down his mouth to the supposed sufferer's ear, and said:

"Don't you feel badly, my friend?"

"Y-y-yes, I do!" said Fraser, without lifting his head. There is no doubt that he *did*, though somewhat more from rum and late hours, than from any religious or moral contrition.

"I thought so!" said the delighted deacon. "I knew you must feel badly, by the way you held down your head. This is a good place you came to, my friend! Don't you think it is good to be here?"

"W-w-well, y-y-yes, rather!" said Bill, "I ha-ha-havn't been in a n-n-nicer place in s-s-some time!" alluding probably to the fact that it promised to be rather a cozy place for a tipsy man to sleep.

"Well, my friend," said the good old deacon, "there is but one thing for you to do! You ought to pray! You *must* pray!"

"D-d-do you th-th-think so?" asked the half-tipsy fellow.

"I am sure of it!" said the deacon.

"W-w-well, you ought to kn-kn-know best!" said the reprobate, "only I'm a little g-g-green and I don't understand m-m-much about it!"

"Try," said the deacon, "and you will be instructed. Fall on your knees at once, and pray!"

"H-h-here's some m-m-more fellows," said the neophyte, indicating his companions. "Th-th-they feel bad too! W-w-what about *them*?"

"Oh," said the deacon, now more than ever hopeful of his convert, "nothing could be better. You show the true feeling—anxiety for your friends. Pray for them."

"W-w-well," said Bill, in a tone and with a manner that would have warned the old deacon if he had been less unsuspicious and absorbed—"w-w-well, if I m-m-ust, I m-m-ust! so h-h-here goes!" and down on his knees he dropped in the pew, and in a voice loud enough to be heard over the whole church, and stop all the other exercises, uttered — no, stuttered—such a prayer as was never heard before or since!

" W-w-we're all sinners, Lord, b-b-but here's some of the cussedest you ever d-d-did see!" By this time he had plenty of auditors.

" H-h-here's B-b-bill Jones, alongside side of me" mentioning the name of one of the fellows with him—" he's g-g-got th-th-three women under w-w-way at once"—symptoms of Jones, furious in face, edging over towards him—" and th-th-there's Tom W-w-wilson," mentioning another close beside him —" if you c-c can d-d-do anything with h-h-him I sh-sh-should like to s-s-see it! H-h-he's the biggest thief in the c-c-country, and can ch-ch-cheat more at division-loo than any t-t-ten men in J-j-jersey!"—

Suddenly something, very probably the fist of the publicly calumniated Tom Wilson, hit Fraser alongside the head, and down he went in the aisle. Before this the deacon had begun to hold up his hands in pious horror at the verbal demon he had unchained, and half the congregation had sprung to their feet and clomb on benches to look over towards the scene of interest. The blow culminated matters. All the rough boys in the back part of the room began to press forward—women screamed and fainted —Fraser, something of a gymnast and bruiser, was on his feet in a moment and paying back the licks with drunken interest—some ran in to drag others out—a few cried " fire!" and " murder!"—fighting became general—and in two minutes that meeting had adjourned itself into the street, in such a row as had probably not before occurred in a religious assemblage since Theodore Hook fastened all the audience down to the benches with awls, in the London church, turned off the gas and bellowed "fire!" and "thieves!"

As fortune would have it, Fraser and his compatriots did not get off scot-free. There was a constable in the assembly, and one of the deacons was a Squire. Fraser was arrested and lugged off to the Squire's house, where he was summarily tried for "disturbing a religious assembly" and had the option of paying down a fine of fifty dollars or going off in a cart to the county jail. He paid down the fifty dollars and was released, while the others escaped with fines of ten dollars each; and it is supposed that they then went back to play out their little interrupted game of loo or poker at the tavern.

Some months elapsed before Bill Fraser was ever again inveigled within the bounds of a religious assemblage. When he did go again, it was also in a country section, to a "protracted meeting," and under circumstances very similar. The same old story—preaching, praying, singing, exhortation. Everybody excited, and everybody apparently happy. Fraser about as tipsy as before, and sitting, as before, with his head down. Another pious old fellow walking down the aisle and appealing to the apparent "mourners." The same fortune as his predecessor had met, led him to accost our neophyte. Nearly the same address, as there is more earnestness than variety in such appeals.

"You are suffering, my friend!"

"W-w-well, I am!" said Bill. "You'd b-b-better believe it!"

"Sin is heavy," said the mentor. "It bows down the head like a bulrush."

"You c-c-can b-b-bet it does!" was the not very

hopeful reply, but the anxious enquirer heeded the matter and not the manner.

"There is balm for every wound," the old man went on.

"S-s-so I have h-h-heard!" said the man with the bowed head.

"But you must do something yourself," said the man of consolation, "or nothing can be done for you."

"W-w-well, g-g-go ahead!" was the answer. "I've b-b-been d-d-doing something all my l-l-life, and if I've g-g-got to d-d-do anything m-m-more, let's h-h-hear from you!"

"My friend," said the comforter, solemnly, "you must *pray*."

"*Pray!*" cried Bill, starting to his feet, eyeing the old deacon very much as if he had caught him with his fingers in his pocket, and blurting out his words so loudly as to throw this second audience into convulsions though happily not into a fight. "*Pray?* N-n-no, I'm c-c-cussed if I do! I t-t-tried that once, and it c-c-cost me f-f-fifty d-d-dollars in l-l-less than h-h-half a minute! I can s-s-stand a l-l little p-p-poker, you know, and a little cut-throat loo, and d-d don't mind t-t-trading horses once in a wh-wh-while, even if they d-d-do cheat me; but I *c-c-can't afford any m-m-more o' that p-p-prayin'—it's altogether too c-c-costly, and too b-b big a luxury for my p-p-pocket-book!*"

Thereupon Bill Fraser stumbled out of church, with the air of a man upon whom a personal injury had been attempted; and as I have since heard of his taking a short term at stone-cutting in government employ, for making a small mistake and putting the wrong man's name to a little piece of paper, it is highly probable that no one ever succeeded in making him a religious proselyte.

XXVII.

HATS AND COATS AT DONATION VISITS.

ONCE upon a time I went to a Donation Visit, in a large town in the country. Does anybody know exactly what a Donation Visit may be? Easily explained: a visit paid in certain country sections annually to the minister of each religious denomination—at which every one is expected to bring something as a present, a supper to be provided, and the visitors to have a good time generally. One brings a cheese—one half a dozen pounds of tea—one the materials for a coat for the pastor or a dress for his wife—one, one to five dollars of the current coin of the republic—one a crock of butter—and so on.

As I was saying, I was inveigled into one of these customary annual parties, and enjoyed it hugely, especially as on such occasions a little more latitude is allowed between the young people than is otherwise considered proper under the minister's roof.

I ought to put in here, in a parenthesis, that Donation Visits sometimes sees displays of execrable meanness perfectly sublime; as when some contemptible sponge brings his wife and three children, stuffs himself and them with a better supper than they have had for a twelvemonth, and give the astounded Domine at parting *half a dollar or a dollar*—about one quarter the value of what they have eaten.

Some rough drollery is there too, occasionally, when "one of the bloods" honors the occasion with his presence, and brings half a dozen pounds of tea or a dozen of butter, snugly packed in a utensil of crockery, all new and clean, but not generally considered appropriate for table use—opens it in full view of all the company, and throws all the men into guffaws, and all the women into blushing like full-blown peonys.

Then the ready-made garments which are sometimes brought and presented—some of them of small size, and highly suggestive, if the minister and his lady happen to be a new-married couple; with the blushing disclaimers, the titterings and the snickerings which follow.

Then, sometimes, when the minister's wife is a shrew, and meaner than any one of her guests—the sport of watching that amiable woman's countenance, while her best carpet is being muddied and her best set of chairs put in peril, without her daring to make an offensive observation. And to watch her when the supper is disappearing somewhat too rapidly, and see the calculations which are made within and show themselves on the surface—as to *whether there will be anything left!*

But all this is foreign to my present reminiscence, to which I must return before the company have dispersed.

At the head of the first flight of stairs was a bedroom, used on that particular occasion as a coat and hat room for the male guests. Every one, on arriving, went up to this retiring-room, and threw his overcoat and hat on the bed, which became, after a time, buried under a pyramid of hats and an avalanche of coats. It is not to be supposed that these articles came out of the heap quite as good as new when the visitors prepared to leave—but no better could be done.

Well—I had occasion to pass the door of this room late in the evening, but before many of the guests had gone. A strapping six-footer from the hills a few miles back of the town was turning over the heap of hats—I could see him through the half-open door—and muttering some things that were not prayers. I had the curiosity to see what was wrong, and so went to the door.

"My hat—where the d——l's my hat?" was his response to my question.

"*Your* hat?" I answered. "What do you mean? are you looking for any particular hat?"

"*My* hat, I tell you!" he replied a little wrathfully, giving the pile of hats another dab, and looking sideways at me. "I want to go home, and can't find my hat!"

"Stranger," said I, determined on a joke, "I don't think you have ever been to one of these parties before."

"No," he answered, "and I don't think I shall ever come to one again."

"Thought you hadn't," I said, "or you wouldn't have been looking for *your hat*, as you call it!"

"Why, what the thunder do you mean?" he asked, turning square around to me.

"Just this, my friend," I said. "You don't seem to know that when people come to these parties, and get ready to go away, the first man *always takes the best hat in the heap that will fit him*, and so they go on down till they finish the heap."

"Oh, that is the way, is it?" he replied.

I went down stairs, content with the prank I had played. So did he, I have no doubt; for he not only took the best hat he could find, but traded his miserable old gloves for a good pair, and his shabby old wrapper for *my overcoat!* I had taught him altogether too much about the morals of Donation Visits!

CPSIA information can be obtained
at www.ICGtesting.com
Printed in the USA
LVHW100446110522
718424LV00003B/260

9 783375 001933